Tailored

FOR Them

CONTENT NOTES:

This story discusses sensitive topics and is meant for readers aged 18 and up. TAILORED FOR THEM contains foul language, explicit content between consenting and enthusiastic adults, feminist themes, discussions of being cheated on (past, off-page), and discussions of parental death (briefly referenced, past, off-page). Readers are advised to decide for themselves if they feel comfortable continuing to read this contemporary romance.

This is a work of fiction. Names, characters, and incidents are products of the author's imagination or are used fictitiously and are not to be construed as real. Any resemblance to actual events, locales, organizations, or persons, living or dead, is entirely coincidental.

FIRST EDITION, 2025

Cover art illustration and design by McKenzie Green

Interior formatting and design by Andrea Andersen

Edits by Yara Gharios

Proofreading by Kelly Andersen

Author's Note

TAILORED FOR THEM is an interconnected novella for two different series. It is both part of the SUN STEER TECH series (taking place a few weeks after MELTED BY A MAN) and the WHAT IT MEANS series (taking place about a decade after WHAT IT MEANS TO BE FOUND).

Knowing this, TAILORED FOR THEM contains quite a few cameos from both series. These cameos are strictly for fun and vibes.

Taylor and Nicole's novella is still a standalone story and can be read by itself without reading any of the other books in the series beforehand.

I hope you fall in love with Taylor and Nicole and their sweet, safe, gentle love for each other, just as I have.

~ Andrea

*To those who have been hurt by someone you loved,
sometimes the best closure is simply moving on*

Chapter One

TAYLOR

MY NAME IS TAYLOR DESMOND, and I was fucking sore.

I took a moment to brace my hands on my knees, inhaling through my nose and exhaling out of my mouth to calm my heart rate. I could smell the saltwater from the nearby ocean in the air. The sound of the waves crashing beyond the grass field I stood on was loud enough for me to focus on for a moment. The sun was setting, painting the cloudless sky in deep warmth. The marine layer was providing a chill in the air, something my sweat-soaked body was struggling to tolerate. My rugby team and I almost had our asses kicked in this last match, but I sprinted like hell to ensure that didn't happen.

I was going to be so fucking stiff tomorrow.

"Good game, T." Leo roughly patted me on the back as he jogged past. His light blue eyes were already on his girlfriend on the sidelines, who held a water bottle in her hands for him. Jacqueline raised a brow as he shook out his inky black hair, grinning as she backed away from him a step. Then another. Soon she was widening her dark brown eyes and grinning from ear to ear, anticipating Leo's moves as he sprinted the last few feet and scooped her up in his sweaty arms. She squealed, playfully hitting his shoulders while he attacked her with kisses to her neck. All of her dark brown hair was tied in a knot on the top of her head, and it fell loose as Leo ravished his girlfriend.

I pulled off my headband and put it back on again, keeping my hair off my face while I turned toward the sound of a man laughing.

My other teammate, Zaid, adjusted his glasses on his nose. He was with his girlfriend and family. He held his nephew, who could be his mini twin. They both shared olive-toned skin and dark hair. Zaid spun his nephew in a circle, making the kid laugh while his girlfriend, Signe, stared at the two of them with hearts in her eyes. She tucked her red hair behind her ears as a grin spread across her cheeks, and she made grabby hands at Zaid's cheeks.

"Taylor!" I heard a child's voice call in the opposite direction. I turned my head to the side and saw Susie Madey excitedly waving me over. I grinned and jogged over to the nine-year-old, who gave me a once-over before loudly proclaiming, "You're stinky."

"Who, me?" I asked, pointing to my cheap jersey and sniffing it, "No. You must be smelling yourself."

Susie wrinkled her nose, her curly blonde hair shaking with her head. "No, trust me. It's you." Her look reminded me so much of her namesake that I felt my chest twist in mourning. Before I could get too in my feelings about that, Susie's dad, and one of my best friends, spoke up.

"Where's the cooler of Gatorade your team gets to dump on you?" Josh, who wore a beanie and sunglasses, attempting to blend in, asked. No one here had recognized the famous rockstar yet, and it had been months since he started bringing Susie to watch me play. I was impressed, but then again, it wasn't uncommon to see celebrities in southern California. Once you've seen enough, the shock and awe start to wear off. Seeing Josh perform live for the first time all those years ago was cool, but the moment Courtney brought him over to hang out with all of us, he was just another guy my friend was dating.

"This isn't football," I rolled my eyes at him as I bent down to pull my water bottle out of my bag, "Plus, no one here would dare try that with me."

I heard a soft, feminine laugh, and my back stiffened at the sound.

When did she show up?

I stood, bringing my water bottle to my lips as I glanced toward the sound that sent my blood pumping, pretending to watch Susie run out onto the field with the rugby ball.

There she was.

Nicole Young.

She stood with Leo and Zaid, and their partners. Whereas Leo and Zaid were my teammates, they were Nicole's coworkers. She was friends with Jacqueline and Signe. The first time I saw her was actually at Signe's apartment a couple of months ago. My friend Eloise wanted to stop by to have Signe sign her romance novel, and I tagged along. That's also how I discovered that one of *my* clients, Violet Thompson, was also an employee at Sun Steer Technologies.

Small world.

Nicole and I didn't talk that night. Eloise and I only stayed for a moment before leaving. But I caught a glimpse of Nicole, sitting on all the pillows and blankets Signe had prepared for their movie night. She tucked her legs close to her body; her arms wrapped around her knees in a hug. She was quiet, observing the scene around her. As soon as my

3

eyes landed on her, Nicole looked away from me and blushed.

She was a stunning woman, even in her pajamas.

I ran into Nicole again when Jacqueline confessed her love to Leo a few weeks ago, and I considered making small talk with her. After watching Nicole watch Jacqueline's performance, I started to become infatuated with the shy, curvy woman. Unfortunately, I got pulled away to help set the large speaker back in Jacqueline's car. The way Nicole smiled and blushed at Jacqueline's dance was endearing.

Our eyes met once, she blushed hard and immediately looked away from me.

When I accidentally bumped into her later, I choked.

She smelled too good. She was so sweet and apologized to me, even though *I* bumped into *her*.

So, yes, I was still very infatuated with her.

I was pretty sure I wanted her.

She had straight, short, almost black hair that hung above her shoulders in a bob. Her dark eyes twinkled at whatever stupid joke Leo probably made, and her lush lips pulled back in a grin that made a dimple pop in her cheek.

I capped my water bottle, caught in her trance.

Like always.

Nicole Young was stunning, even just wearing khaki shorts and sneakers, a plain t-shirt that would barely be able to keep her warm from the ocean breeze dancing across the field.

It showed off the tattoos on her arms. Inky butterflies were scattered on her bicep. The raccoon with the bouquet of flowers. I tossed my water bottle back in the bag, my head still turned so I didn't miss a moment of her. I blindly reached for my sweat rag and wrapped it around my shoulders, dabbing at my neck and chest as I watched

Nicole toss her head back and laugh again. The sound echoed across the grass.

The group over there turned, headed in my direction. Probably to discuss how great the game went with me, but I couldn't pretend I wasn't staring at *her*.

I didn't even try to hide it, I never did.

Because half the time she caught me staring at her, I was gifted with the sight of her cheeks darkening with a blush. I *lived* for that moment.

"...and then Court stuck her thirty-two-ounce Hydro flask up my ass." Josh's words made me blink and startle back into the moment.

"What the fuck?" I asked him.

"Oh, are you listening to me now?" He raised an eyebrow, lined with two piercings as he smirked, and his eyes danced across the field to the group heading toward us, "Which one are you staring at, T?"

I shook my head, "No one."

"Is it the Englishman? I get it," Josh raised his eyebrows as he admired Leo with a low whistle, "Accents."

"Nope." I shook my head once, glancing up to see them getting closer.

"The brunette?"

I froze, glaring at him. He widened his eyes as a shit-eating grin spread across his cheeks, "Which one? Long hair, or short?"

I glanced back at the sound of her laugh again, making direct eye contact this time. As soon as our eyes met, her smile lost a little bit of its boldness.

I wondered why.

She glanced to the side where Jacqueline was talking with her, but her dark eyes landed on me again, and it felt like a gust of wind was about to knock me off my feet. And then there it was, the pink that stained her cheeks whenever we made eye contact. I hoped, deep down, that meant she liked what she saw.

My friends often called me a flirt, and I couldn't argue with them. There is casual flirting, which I'd argue wasn't true flirting, but was more messing around with my close friends. And then there was flirting-flirting, when I tried to make it obvious that I was sexually interested in a person.

Being pansexual meant that I didn't care what someone's gender was; I'd dated men, women, and other enbies. I was mostly attracted to people's vibes.

Nicole Young's vibes made something swoop in my lower belly, and my heart picked up its pace.

I just hoped she might reciprocate.

I felt safe using dating apps. The app made it clear where everyone stood. They could read my bio, see they/them pronouns under my name, see some pictures of myself to ensure I was their type, and everyone could get together with proper expectations.

Meeting someone in the wild like this? Through happenstance? A friend of a friend? It required some sleuthing on my part. I didn't know a lot about her—*yet*—and I hadn't confirmed if she was queer or not. Perhaps her bob and her raccoon tattoo were giveaways, but I generally didn't ramp up my charm unless I knew for sure. There was no queer coded keychain or carabiner that I could see on her person, just a fanny pack looped across her torso. I needed to take time to figure this out, because the closer she approached, the more I felt my attraction toward her heart-shaped face and dark eyes, and soft smile rise.

God, her *smile*.

My favorite was when she smiled widely, creating soft smile lines on her cheeks.

I always gravitated toward people shorter than me. I also loved a feminine, curvy body. And Nicole had plenty of that.

"We're going out for celebratory drinks," Leo said, tucking Jacqueline closer to his side. I nodded a silent hello to his girlfriend as they finally reached where Josh and I stood. I didn't bother with formal introductions between Josh and the others, in an attempt to conceal Josh's identity as much as I could. However, people usually figured out who he was after talking with him.

"Where at?" I asked, sliding my towel off my neck and dabbing it on my forehead. I always sweated a ton after a game of rugby.

I glanced over at Nicole, who stood on Jacqueline's other side and watched me dab my skin with a focused expression. Good focus? Bad focus? Who the hell knew? I could practically feel her eyes on me, though.

"Two blocks away," Leo pointed in the general direction behind me, and I nodded.

"Sorry, unfortunately—"

"Taylor would love to go," Josh said, standing beside me and wrapping one of his long arms around my shoulders. "I'm Josh, what are your names?"

I guessed Josh wasn't worried about these people recognizing him.

"Leo," The Englishman, as Josh referred to him, held his hand out for him to shake, "This is my partner, Jacqueline." Josh shook her hand too, nodding with a polite smile behind his sunglasses, "And this is Nicole. We all work together."

"Where do you work?" Josh asked, shaking Nicole's hand last and dropping it. I crossed my arms, determined not to look embarrassed or uncomfortable with Josh's obvious prying.

"Sun Steer Technologies," Nicole replied.

"With the solar-powered, self-steering tractors," Susie chimed in, tossing the ball carelessly in the air, "A boy in my class just did his report on them."

"No shit," Josh raised his eyebrows behind his glasses, "That's where you work? That technology is insane." Josh emphasized his point by making an exploding sound with his mouth and gesturing with his hand near his head.

"See that guy over there?" Nicole gave Josh a conspiratorial look as she pointed to Zaid, "He's the one who built most of the software."

"Wow," Josh stared at my teammate for a moment before glaring down at me, "You didn't tell me your rugby team had cool fucking people on it."

I also didn't tell them that the most famous rock star in the world regularly attended our rugby matches with his daughter. But, whatever.

I shrugged, "My bad."

"Don't say 'fuck' so much," Susie scolded her dad, tossing the ball in the air again, "It's lazy."

Everyone's eyes widened at the nine-year-old dropping the f-bomb. Except mine, of course. After being friends with Josh and Courtney for over a decade, I was used to the way they parented their daughter.

"You're right," Josh nodded. He reached into his pocket and pulled out a dollar bill to hand to his daughter. She didn't even make eye contact as she reached her hand out for him to slap it in her palm. She pocketed the bill with ease before turning to me with wide eyes.

"Want to pass with me for a bit?"

"T is gonna go get drinks with their team, Suse," Josh stepped forward, holding his arms up, "But I'll pass with you."

"T can speak for themself," I replied with a lifted eyebrow.

"T needs to go celebrate with the team like a good team captain." Josh lifted his middle finger at me behind his back so his daughter couldn't see.

"This is getting tense," Leo murmured, lowering his head toward Jacqueline's ear.

"Please don't feel pressured to come." That was Nicole's voice, and if I had ears like a dog or something, they would have perked right up: "There's always next time." Nicole looked down at the ground after she spoke, making me suspect that she was nervous to speak up.

But she was talking to me directly, which didn't happen often.

So, I was joining her.

"No, no," I shook my head, pulling my jersey from myself and cringing from the reek of it, "Shit, I smell like ass, though."

"I told you," Susie chimed in before tossing the ball to Josh.

"We all do," Leo emphasized his point by tugging Jacqueline closer to his body. She wrinkled her nose in disgust while pulling away from him.

"Good point," I lifted a shoulder, trying to find the calm, cool, confident Taylor that I usually am, "I'm down. Bye, nerds." I turned back to Susie and Josh, still tossing the rugby ball back and forth, and lifted my fingers in a parting peace sign.

Susie returned the gesture, but Josh caught the ball and held it as he asked, "You're still good for Saturday?"

I gave him a thumbs up as I bent down to scoop up my bag, "More than ready."

"Bring Nerf guns!" Susie called again. I gave her a

thumbs up too, before turning toward Leo and the women to follow them off the field.

"...What are you doing Saturday?" Jacqueline asked as she blindly reached for Leo's hand. I remembered a while back when Leo and I chatted about possible ways to help Jacqueline during that time. As he described Jacqueline to me, my internal *neurodivergent person radar* was going off. Based on how well she responded to the advice I gave Leo; I was under the impression that I was correct.

"Babysitting," I replied, adjusting to shoulder my bag. I walked next to Nicole, and I really wished that I had a chance to shower or something instead. She smelled amazing. Something floral, and I couldn't tell if it was perfume or shampoo, or deodorant. All I knew was that I wanted to lean in and absorb myself in it.

But I didn't do that, because I'm not a creep.

I stayed a respectable distance away, walking side-by-side with the others, and kept my cool.

"That girl needs a babysitter?" Leo asked, glancing over his shoulder to where we left Susie and Josh.

"Not really," I admitted, "But her baby brother, and our friends' five-year-old and her baby brother do."

I saw Jacqueline wince, "That sounds like a lot."

I grinned, "The babies are relatively easy, as long as they're fed and played with. The five-year-old tries to be in charge of everyone, though."

"That's cute," Nicole's lips lifted in a smile as she stared ahead to where we were walking, and I wished deep in my bones that she would direct it toward me. But no, I smelled like sweat, so I knew I wouldn't be my *most* flirtatious self today.

No, if I were going to go out of my way to flirt with Nicole, I wanted to be showered. Fresh.

I also needed to determine if she *wanted* me to flirt with her, which was weirdly difficult for me to do for some reason. I felt like I was in my early twenties, navigating the dating scene for the first time, instead of my late thirties; someone who had dated the ish out of almost every queer person in Orange County.

"Babies scare me," Jacqueline murmured.

"Not me," I replied.

"That's right," Leo perked up, stepping ahead of us with Jacqueline as the sidewalk narrowed. We were walking in pairs now, and I both preened and cringed at the thought of Nicole being stuck walking next to smelly me, "T works with babies every day."

I nodded, "From the age of twelve months to three years old."

Nicole turned to look up at me, her dark eyes scanning my face as she asked her question, "What do you do for work?"

"I'm an occupational therapist," I faced forward, attempting to conceal my blush from such close, direct eye contact with her, "I work with children who have delays. I help them get up to speed and teach their parents how to support them better."

I glanced back down at Nicole, and my heart thumped in my chest from being in such close proximity to her.

Nicole widened her eyes, her lip turned up in the corner, "That's so cool."

Not as cool as being a CFO at Sun Steer, I thought to myself, but hey, I'd take it.

"It's fun," I grinned, allowing myself one bold once over. How would she feel in my hands? She had soft curves, curves that I wanted to grab and hold and pull into myself. The flare of her hips under those khaki shorts called to me.

Would Nicole like my touch? I made a mental note in my head tonight to determine if Nicole was queer. And if she was, how queer was she? I started creating a list of queer bands and movies to ask her about, to see how she reacted to them.

Her short fingernails looked promising, though.

Nicole snapped her head forward, and I scolded myself for being so bold and checking her out.

You still smell like ass, T, I reminded myself as I faced forward.

"Here we are," Leo announced, holding the door open to a small local bar. He was a gentleman and held it open for everyone, but I still gestured for Nicole to step ahead of me with Jacqueline.

The noise of the bar sucked me out of my lustful fantasies of my teammate's co-worker, and I gave myself one more mental talking-to before following everyone to the bar and ordering a drink.

Just a *little* bit of flirting today.

I was here to hang out with my teammate, his girlfriend, and their coworker.

Nothing sexual.

Nothing presumptuous.

Then I would go home and promptly shower and grab my toy until I saw stars.

Chapter Two

NICOLE

I FUCKING LOVE GUACAMOLE.

My ex-girlfriend always rolled her eyes at that fact, calling me basic and encouraging me to branch out. Colleen was a certified food snob, and because Mexican food was such a common and exceptional cuisine in southern California, she was determined to find other, more niche foods to try and praise.

Whereas I could eat Mexican food every day for the rest of my life and be happy.

I *really* wanted to feel happy.

Whatever that looked like.

A sharp pain stabbed me in my lungs unexpectedly, which happened more often than I'd like. My ex always snuck into my mind, even after so much time had passed. Small things triggered the memories. Whenever I had to work late at my dream job. Whenever I came home with some flowers that I thought were cute and bought myself. Eating the greatest food on the planet because only a very bitter, sad person could hate guac as much as she did.

At least I finally had the opportunity to create financial

stability while working at Sun Steer, because the company paid the best out of any tech startup in southern California.

I had to remind myself of the silver linings, no matter how small they were. I had been alone for so long. This was due to a number of reasons. One being that my parents passed, and I was an only child with no additional family nearby.

I had been feeling very much abandoned and unsupported during, what I would argue, was one of the most isolated chapters of my adult life. This was why I was trying to tag along with my co-workers to non-work things more often, desperate to stop mourning my last relationship.

I needed my *own* group of people. I needed my own friends outside of whatever relationship I found myself in next. I needed a foundation of support, so I wouldn't find myself feeling abandoned if I experienced another breakup.

Shaking myself out of my spiraling thoughts, I scooped another chip of guac and shoved it in my mouth.

Happiness.

"Should we get another bowl?" Taylor asked.

Taylor.

I gave them a sheepish grin around my full bite, desperate to keep my lips closed.

Taylor Desmond was painfully attractive, and I had never felt more intimidated by a person in my life.

During the game, I kept watching Taylor whenever they adjusted their headband. Their brown hair was thick and voluminous, mostly because they kept brushing their fingers through it. When I first met them, they had little designs shaved into the back of their head. Now, though, I noticed that their hair had grown out a bit.

It looked a little messier.

Sometimes, I wanted to mess it up even more.

Their eyes were a deep, dark blue as they raised their dark brows at me, because I hadn't answered their question yet. Their dark eyelashes fanned with their waiting blink. When their smirk turned into a grin, I tried not to imagine what their full lips would taste like.

Their septum piercing was a gold ring today, and it twitched with their smile as they raised their hand to ask a passing waiter for another serving of guacamole.

Taylor didn't even wait for my response.

They just got me more.

I usually gravitated toward femme-presenting women, like Colleen. Every long-term relationship I had been in was with femme women. I hadn't dated anyone who dressed more masc and gender neutral, like Taylor. I had no idea how to flirt with them.

What would flirting with Taylor look like?

What would intimacy with Taylor look like? I'd pictured it many times since the first time I saw them at Signe Lange's apartment. How their lean body would feel over mine. How the line of muscle on their stomach would taste under my tongue. The things they'd whisper to me.

I first met Taylor weeks ago at a girls' night I attended at Signe's apartment. They had shown up with another friend of Signe's, only briefly, and the studio apartment suddenly felt too small.

It was the first time I felt attracted to someone since my breakup.

I didn't think Taylor noticed me that night. There was some drama unfolding, and they quickly excused themselves to let us brainstorm with Jacqueline about what to do for Leo. But then Taylor and I officially met later at

Laguna field, when they set up a speaker for Jacqueline to use while she danced her love for Leo.

Violet, another coworker of ours, also already knew Taylor. Her daughter had worked with them for a few years. So, when they brought up the fact that they were an occupational therapist earlier, I already knew about that.

I realized then that I probably shouldn't pursue anything with them. Our friend circles were already too intertwined. If we started dating and broke up, I could lose these friendships I'd made with my coworkers. Our workdays could end up tense and weird. Uncomfortable. I didn't want to risk losing what friendships I barely had over a broken romantic relationship *again*.

Obviously, this was assuming that Taylor reciprocated any attraction toward me. This was also assuming that their hypothetical attraction could lead to something more, because in my big fat romantic brain, attraction *always* led to big feelings and love confessions.

But I enjoyed talking with Taylor, because I appreciated the sound of their voice. It was a warm, soft voice that soothed me.

However, I was fresh out of the mourning stage of my breakup. Just barely considering putting myself out there again. Taylor, however, seemed so confident in a way I couldn't put into words. It was almost too intimidating, but against my better judgment, they thrilled me. I wasn't sure if it was my hormones taking over or if it was my personal intuition, but Taylor seemed like the kind of person who knew *exactly* what they were doing in the bedroom.

I wondered if they triggered this visceral reaction in everyone around them, or if it was just me.

Was I ready for someone like Taylor Desmond?

Definitely not, I thought to myself.

"Here you go," the waiter returned with a fresh bowl of guac, and I sat straighter in my seat. We were all sharing a four-person table, each of us taking a side.

"Let me just—" Taylor had a smile on their face as they swapped out the half-eaten bowl of guac in front of me and replaced it with the full one.

Embarrassment immediately flooded my cheeks, "Oh, that's okay, I don't—"

"Please," Taylor shook their head, their dark blue eyes dragged over me in a way that heated my core, "Have at it."

I pressed my lips together, glancing at Leo and Jacqueline, who also seemed happy to finish off the half-empty bowl while I started on the fresh one.

"Thanks," I murmured before accepting my fate. I was more than willing to fill up on guac in between sips from my margarita. I took a drink, trying to focus back on the conversation.

"I still don't understand," Jacqueline frowned. Leo and Taylor were desperately trying to explain to her what "scrum" was in the game. I was confused too, because I knew nothing about rugby. Leo tried connecting it to software development scrums, like what the engineers at work did.

But Jacqueline was in HR, and I was the CFO.

We weren't involved in any program development at all.

So, we were still lost.

Taylor started grabbing bottles of hot sauce to explain what had happened during their match, and I grinned before the sound of laughter sent cold chills down my spine.

I knew that high-pitched laugh.

Colleen was here.

I froze with a chip halfway to my mouth.

She was off to the side somewhere, and my head

swiveled in her direction before I could stop myself. Colleen and Sarah were at the bar, sipping cocktails and having a great time together.

Shit.

Fuck.

Shit-fuck.

I lowered my chip, suddenly sick to my stomach.

Memories of the last night we were together flooded my brain.

"I was lonely," she told me, when I found her in bed with another woman that evening, "What did you expect from me?"

I don't know, maybe a conversation about your feelings instead of sabotaging a year-long relationship with me? I wasn't getting any younger, and I wanted to find my person and be settled. I wanted to have someone to have fun with during my retirement. My parents never had that, because they had to work until the day they died.

Colleen knew how lonely *I* was.

She had "won" all our mutual friends in the breakup, because they were her friends first.

They were *still* together. All these months later, Colleen and Sarah were still obviously together. Seeing my ex and the woman she left me for made me want to disappear. I wished for a hole to open up under my chair and swallow me into the ground.

"Whoa, you good?" Taylor paused their rugby explanation and leaned toward me, making Jacqueline and Leo look at me too.

"Yeah," I nodded, then turned and saw Colleen and Sarah lean forward to share a quick kiss. I shook my head, "No. Crap. I'm sorry." I slammed my elbows down on the table and shielded my face with my hand. "My ex is over there."

"Again?" Leo turned to Jacqueline, "Does this pub send out a signal to everyone's exes?" Jacqueline shrugged at his comment. I had no idea what they were talking about, but I peeked under my hand to see what they were up to. I couldn't look away from Colleen. She was beautiful, with natural blonde hair and a body to kill for. Legs for miles. Her makeup was always flawless and looked natural enough to fool most people. Sarah was just as stunning, wearing a jean skirt with sneakers and a crop top that showed off a belly-button ring. Her red hair was casually braided away from her heart-shaped face.

Suddenly, perhaps feeling my eyes on her, Colleen turned toward our table. I hid my face with my hand before we made eye contact, "Shit, is she looking over here?" I murmured at the table.

Taylor covertly glanced over their shoulder and checked, "The blonde? Yeah. She keeps looking over here."

"Fuck me," I whispered, "I should go."

"What? No. Assert your dominance." Leo gently pounded his fist on the table. "We were here first."

"Were we?" Jacqueline asked him.

"I don't know, but I feel like we were," Leo shrugged, "Just breathe. Was it a bad breakup?"

"Terrible," I murmured, keeping my hand locked on the side of my face, "She cheated on me with the redhead. I didn't know they were still together." Heat flamed my cheeks, and something was burning in my chest. I shook my head, "I don't want her to see me shaken like this."

"Hey," Taylor reached out and wrapped one of their hands on my shoulder, squeezing me, "You're okay. She sucks. You have no reason to be embarrassed. She should be the one embarrassed." I lifted my eyes to meet theirs, seeing only sincerity in their expression. My heart started thumping in my chest from the feel of their warm hand on my shoulder, and I gave them a tentative smile in thanks.

"Shit," Leo murmured, crouching low toward the table, "I think she's coming over here."

"No," I wheezed, "No, no, no. She's going to know."

"Know what?" Taylor asked as a pinch formed between their dark brows.

"That I've been a mess ever since," I felt my chin wobble, "That she broke a small piece of me." The admission was embarrassing, but I didn't regret admitting it either. I felt safe with my friends here. I wasn't scared for them to know exactly how shitty this breakup had been.

Taylor glanced over their shoulder, "They're definitely talking about coming over here." Taylor glanced down at the table before looking at Jacqueline and Leo. All three of them exchanged panicked looks, trying to come up with something to help.

I had great friends.

"Just pretend you're completely over her," Leo murmured, his light blue eyes checking over toward the bar, "As if you didn't even notice she was here."

I snorted, "How?"

"Look focused on something else." Jacqueline lifted a shoulder, "Pretend we're talking about something intriguing."

"Besides my cheating ex having the ovaries to come over here?" I muttered.

Taylor grinned, "I'm great with exes."

I huffed a laugh, "What does that even mean?"

Taylor's eyes dropped toward my lips, which parted against their own volition. As if Taylor's attention on my lips hypnotized them, "Do you trust me?" Taylor asked, meeting my eyes again.

I blinked at them, lowering my hand a fraction, "Um. I think so."

"If I cross a line, kick me under the table," Taylor pulled off their headband and quickly ran their fingers through their dark hair, giving their hair more volume, and swooping it up and to the side. They styled it in a way that made me want to run my fingers through their hair myself.

"Okay?" I asked it like a question right before Taylor reached over and grabbed a leg of my chair, and roughly scooted me much, much closer to them. It made a loud scrape against the tile flooring, and I braced myself by gripping the edge of the table so I wouldn't accidentally fall into their lap.

"I know I smell like ass, but let me help," I felt Taylor's breath on my cheek and neck. They draped one of their arms on the back of my chair, and I shivered at the feel of their warm lips brushing against my temple. I realized what they were doing, what they were setting up the scene to look like. I met Leo's enthusiastic grin before I turned to face Taylor, who was so, so close to me.

I was about to say something, but Taylor turned their head to keep their lips near my ear as they continued, "Keep your attention on me as much as you can. Right now, you're not her ex. You're mine, Nicole."

I gasped, my eyes wide, and a blush stained my cheeks. Leo chuckled as he took a sip from his beer, and Jacqueline pushed the new guac bowl in front of Taylor and me.

Taylor's fingers gently brushed my arm, creating a wave of goosebumps and a shiver that came from being this close to their warm body.

"Nic?" I stiffened at the old nickname, my nervous

system a complete wreck from the exhilarating experience of sitting in Taylor Desmond's embrace while hearing my ex's voice.

Taylor murmured, "Don't turn yet," in my ear before they brushed their lips across my temple, a delicate touch that left a scorching path. My lips parted. I was pretty sure I was panting. I lowered my hand from the table to wrap my fingers around Taylor's thigh. I meant the touch to be some type of grounding gesture, a signal that I was out of my element and had no idea how to navigate this. But their hand covered mine, squeezing against my fingers and encouraging my touch on their leg.

And their other hand? Fingers skimmed my arm and across my shoulder, teasing my neck and traveling to my hairline.

I shivered, and I felt Taylor's lips pull back in a smile on my temple before they leaned back to look at me.

I not so subtly leaned into their touch, my heart hammering in my chest because I couldn't remember the last time someone touched me like this. I missed it. I wanted it.

"Nicole," Colleen cleared her throat, and I widened my eyes at Taylor. They smirked before their dark blue eyes shifted to look up at my ex over my shoulder.

"Someone's trying to talk to you, babe," Taylor nodded in Colleen's direction. My cheeks flamed with the term of endearment, something that Taylor's eyes clocked, if the way they lowered and dragged back and forth over my face had any indication.

They had just single-handedly created the perfect ruse.

They were my partner.

I was theirs.

But what did I call them?

Taylor just called me "babe."

Should I call them "babe" back? I didn't think I had ever called anyone "babe". I wasn't a pet name person, but I couldn't ignore the butterflies that took off in my stomach from hearing Taylor refer to me as "babe".

I was panicking.

This is fake, Nicole, I reminded myself.

"Huh?" I asked, blinking while I studied the way Taylor licked their bottom lip.

"Behind you," Taylor replied before they leaned in, gently brushing their nose against mine to whisper, "You're doing great."

I exhaled my breath on a wheeze when they pulled back, before finally turning my head to look up at Colleen.

She was...stunning. As always.

But my heart was underwhelmed by her proximity. I could feel Taylor's fingers gently massaging my neck underneath my hair, a physical reminder that I wasn't alone. That they were making me flushed and flustered right now, not Colleen.

"Oh," I grinned up at her, "Hi."

Colleen smiled, but her eyes were darting between me and Taylor with an odd look, "How are you? It's been forever." She opened her arms wide, and I wanted to scream. Was that really how she was playing this? As if the last time we saw each other, she hadn't taken my heart and shattered it into a million pieces? As if I didn't watch her and Sarah practically skip out of the door of our apartment?

I tried not to grimace before I stood from my seat, immediately missing Taylor's grounding touch, and gave her the briefest, stiffest hug I had ever given someone.

Taylor wasn't wrong, they were sweaty after playing rugby with Leo earlier this afternoon. But after smelling

Colleen's familiar perfume, I wanted nothing more than to be surrounded again by Taylor's natural scent mixed with fresh-cut grass and whatever body spray they put on before the game.

It was citrusy, a smell I didn't normally lean toward but found appealing on them.

I was about to take my seat again when Colleen's hand wrapped around my wrist, keeping me standing with her and Sarah. Sarah looked more uncomfortable than Colleen did, but managed to pull her lips into a stiff, friendly smile.

"What have you been up to? Are you still working at..." Colleen snapped her fingers, unable to remember the name of the company she previously blamed for pushing her to cheat on me.

My hands balled into fists at my sides, but I did my best to maintain a friendly smile.

"Sun Steer. And yes, I'm still there," I practically spoke through gritted teeth.

"Right!" Colleen's eyes widened. "How's that been going?"

"Good," I nodded, "I still love it."

Colleen's smile wavered a little before she released my hand and looped her arm through Sarah's, "I'm glad to hear it, we've—"

"—Taylor?" Sarah leaned around me, her green eyes widening as she addressed my fake partner, "Oh my god, I thought I recognized you."

Back off, they're mine.

Thankfully, I didn't speak the impulsive thought out loud.

"Oh, hi!" The sound of metal scraping along the tile let me know Taylor was standing to properly greet the woman who swiftly stole Colleen from me. I stepped to the side, letting them wrap Sarah up in a quick hug, before they stepped back and took up space beside me.

"Do you come here often?" Sarah asked, squeezing Colleen's arm against her side.

"It's my first time, actually," Taylor grinned casually at Sarah, and right when my eyeballs were darting between the two of them, wondering what their history was, there was a tug on one of the beltloops of my khaki shorts.

As soon as my side pressed up against Taylor's again, I realized that they had just casually used their finger to pull me into their embrace.

Their hand rested on my opposite hip, and I found myself squeezing it against me in response. The flex of their fingers over my shirt both soothed and excited me.

"Nicole was telling me about their guac, so we decided to meet up here." Taylor's fingers accidentally dragged my shirt up a hair, exposing the smallest sliver of my midriff. Their pinky brushed against my skin, and when my breath caught in my throat, they froze their movements.

"Oh, is this your partner?" Colleen asked, holding a hand toward Taylor for them to shake.

Sarah gave us both a sheepish grin before turning to her girlfriend, lowering her voice so only the four of us could hear, "Oh, no. Taylor doesn't have partners. They have flings."

I felt my heart sink low, low into my gut.

I wanted to die.

Taylor didn't *have* partners.

I wasn't a fling kind of girl. I was a romantic once upon a time. I wanted the commitment. I was a big ol' fan of monogamy.

Colleen knew this about me. There was no chance that I was suddenly okay with a casual situationship and based on the raised brow and sad smile she gave me, I had a feeling she was slowly realizing how fake this relationship with Taylor was.

Fucking fuck.

"That was true at one point, yes." Taylor nodded, squeezing me to their side, "But that was before I met Nicole."

I held my breath right when their soft, warm lips pressed firmly against the crown of my head. I could almost feel their septum ring nudge my head as well. I knew for a fact that my face was flaming.

Based on the way Sarah stiffened, her lips parting in visible shock from Taylor's words, I wanted to point a finger in her face and yell, "HA-HA, Taylor picked me and not you! You can't have them!"

But I didn't.

Colleen's brows lifted after seeing Sarah's reaction, "Really?"

"I mean, can you blame me?" Taylor laughed, using their free hand to tuck a strand of my hair behind my ear, letting the cool air hit my blazing hot cheek, "I tried to wear her down, but you know Nicole." Taylor gave Colleen a look as if they were both in on some kind of well-known knowledge about me. Based on the way Colleen nodded, I realized exactly what Taylor meant earlier when they said they were good with exes. "She wasn't about to settle. Either I needed to step up and be with her or let her seriously date other people. But I couldn't just let a woman like her go."

I blushed at their words, knowing it was all a lie, but they warmed my heart regardless. "Stop it." I rolled my eyes and gave Taylor a playful shove. They responded by taking a finger and tracing the shape of my jaw, before turning my head to face them directly.

Their expression was soft; their deep blue eyes darted between both of mine in what I later realized was a check-in before they pecked the tip of my nose with their lips.

I practically swooned.

"...You, Taylor Desmond, are monogamously dating one person?" Sarah lifted an incredulous eyebrow, her lips stiff in a way that reminded me how I felt a few moments ago, "Really?"

"I can't believe it either," I gave Sarah a wide-eyed look, "It still feels like I'm dreaming."

"But Taylor doesn't seem like your usual type," Colleen was practically frowning now.

I froze.

Taylor froze.

How dare she?

"Excuse me?" I asked.

"It's just—" Colleen shrugged her shoulders, her facial expression much less amused as she studied the two of us, "They don't seem like your type. You've always liked femmes, Nic."

Like her, she meant.

I gaped, ready to rip into Colleen for being an insecure mean girl when Taylor squeezed me against them once more and murmured, "Wow. At least Nicole had the decency to wait until I was comfortable bringing up my gender identity myself."

Behind us, I thought I heard Leo snort.

"*You* can call me Nicole." I reached over and wrapped an arm around Taylor's waist, too, trying to claim them as much as they were claiming me right now, "And you have no idea what my type is."

"We dated for a year," Colleen gave me a sad, fake smile, "I know you."

27

"I'm sorry," Taylor lifted a hand between us, "You're telling me that you had this goddess of a woman for a year, and you still managed to fuck it up? What did you do?" Then they looked directly at Sarah, and I held in a gasp.

Colleen's jaw dropped, and Sarah glanced down as an embarrassed flush stained her cheeks.

"I think we should get back to our friends," I gestured behind me, where Jacqueline and Leo sat watching this train wreck of a conversation, "It was...something, seeing you." I went to pull Taylor with me, encouraging the two of us to return to our seats.

"I didn't mean to offend you," Colleen stepped forward, ignoring when Taylor and I sat down. She practically towered over us, "I'm just surprised to see you with someone like...them." She was blushing, and it took me a second to realize it, but Colleen was embarrassed.

Not me, Colleen.

As she fucking should be.

"Well, you *did* offend me. And Taylor." I rested my hand on their thigh again, and they returned their arm to the back of my chair. "You lost the right to know anything about me or my partners as soon as you brought another person into our bed without my consent. Goodbye."

Leo let out a low whistle, and Taylor silently took a sip of their beer. Everyone at the table was looking at Colleen and Sarah, the former slowly inching away as if she wanted to escape.

Colleen opened her mouth again, but I turned away.

Not toward our friends, but to Taylor specifically.

They had just placed their bottle of beer on the tabletop before turning to face me too, a delighted sparkle in their eyes that quickly morphed into surprise when both of my hands cupped their face.

Then, without any warning, I pulled their mouth to mine.

Thankfully, they responded. Taylor's arm wrapped around my shoulders while their other hand gripped my waist. It was a little awkward, sitting directly next to them in our chairs, but we both leaned into it.

It wasn't an explicit kiss by any means.

In an odd sort of way, I wanted to thank them with it.

Their soft, warm lips gently brushed and nipped against mine. No tongues were involved at all, even though I desperately wanted to taste them.

I slid one of my hands into the back of their head, their short, half-shaven strands molded between my fingers in a way that made me sigh against their mouth.

The kiss lasted no more than a few seconds tops, and when we pulled back from each other, I was rewarded with a faint, pink blush staining each of Taylor Desmond's cheeks. Their eyes were hooded, and their dark pupils expanded to conceal most of the blue of their eyes.

I lifted my hand to my own lip, tracing where I could still feel theirs.

"They're gone," Leo grinned, making the two of us snap out of whatever trance we were in and pull completely away from each other, "Fucking hell, that was brilliant."

Chapter Three

TAYLOR

IF THERE WAS one thing that I took away from the night I had drinks with Leo, Jacqueline, and Nicole, it was that Nicole's kisses were practically drugging.

She was an excellent kisser.

I had kissed many, many people in my life.

In my early twenties, I went through a hoe phase, just as any other person does. I wasn't unfamiliar with kissing. I had it down to a science. Kissing was an art I had perfected over time. Something as second nature to me as breathing.

But kissing Nicole Young in that taco bar the other day?

I felt like a virgin again.

And I didn't even believe in the social construct of virginity.

A Nerf dart pinged me in the head, and I was immediately pulled out of my thoughts. I blinked back into the present, pushing the haunting memory of Nicole's soft hands holding my face to hers, to see Iris St. James standing above me, holding a Nerf gun right at my forehead.

She had found my hiding spot, which wasn't hard to do since I was just crouching behind the couch.

"Gotchya," she grinned, an evil sneaky grin that could have been copied and pasted onto her face from her mother's. Perhaps it was the freckles they shared.

"Darn," I shook my head, standing up to accept my defeat, "I need to hide better. You're too good at this."

"Wait!" The five-year-old lifted her hands as her wide eyes flitted around the living room, "Let's pretend you're on my team now."

"Okay!" I crouched low, following her to the other side of the living room and hiding behind one of the ancient, ugly accent chairs that had existed for decades before Iris was even a thought.

Upstairs, we heard Susie stomping around.

"Are you ready?" I lifted my own Nerf gun and set it on top of the chair, hiding most of my body from view. Iris leaned to the side, closing one eye and aiming at the end of the staircase as if she were lining up a shot using a scope.

"Ready, Freddy." She replied.

The two of us held our breath as we waited for Susie to hop down the stairs. She was humming a song of some kind, completely lost in her thoughts.

Poor kid didn't stand a chance.

As soon as she came into view, Iris and I unloaded our Nerf guns.

Susie immediately laughed and lifted her hands to shield herself, before accepting her fate and dramatically pretending to die. She clutched her stomach, tipping precariously from side to side, moaning and gargling.

Iris was cackling throughout the whole performance.

Eventually, Susie fell to her knees, wailing and gasping, before falling face-forward onto the hardwood floor.

Damn, get this girl into Hollywood.

"We won!" Iris cheered, dropping her gun to hold both of her fists in the air.

I scooped Iris up and managed a very awkward victory lap around the living room, before plopping the two of us back onto the worn yellow couch.

The townhome had changed a lot since Courtney and Josh moved in, but through years of determination, Courtney was able to maintain the old furniture by reupholstering them with identical fabrics and learning how to rebuild the framework by watching a ton of YouTube videos.

Courtney Madey was very sentimental about the ugly accent chairs and yellow couch, but the rest of the townhome felt updated.

Susie giggled before pushing herself up and resting on her knees, "The babies are asleep." She announced. Susie was obsessed with her baby brother, the little guy less than a year old. She helped Courtney feed, burp, and rock the little man to sleep. She even demanded that she be the one to feed him his first solid food, pureed carrots.

Iris, however, often forgot that she even had a baby brother. The boys were only a few weeks apart in age.

"Thanks for checking on them," I sighed to Susie, stretching my neck out.

The doorknob to the front of the house started jiggling, and Iris quickly turned her head to look at me. Her dark curls, so similar to her dad's, swung with the movement. Her eyes were wide, and her lips were pulled down in a dramatic frown.

"No, I don't want you to leave yet!" Iris cried.

"This is my house, you're the one leaving," Susie corrected, standing up and racing toward the entryway.

When Logan St. James filled the doorway, followed by his wife, Eloise, Susie sighed.

"Oh, it's just you."

"Damn," Eloise laughed, scrunching her freckled nose, "Sorry to disappoint."

"How was it?" I asked them as I stood from the couch. Suddenly, Iris latched her arms and legs around my calf. I found myself dragging the five-year-old with me as I shuffled to greet her parents.

"It was good, thanks again for watching everyone," Eloise smiled as she moved to the side, letting Susie race out the door and down the porch steps.

"Of course," I grinned down at her daughter, giggling as I pretended to be unaffected by her koala-bear grip on my leg, "I had fun with these crazies."

"More fun than you would have had at the orchestra?" Eloise asked with a lifted blonde eyebrow. Her parents had gifted everyone with tickets, and as cool as orchestras were, I preferred babysitting for my friends instead of sitting through a boring-as-hell performance.

"That's not even a question."

I grinned when the sound of Susie's laughter echoed through the front door. Dark curls fell over Logan's forehead while he crouched to try to untangle his daughter's limbs from my leg. Meanwhile, Joshua Madey marched through his doorway with Susie slung over his shoulder like a sack of potatoes.

"You think you're *so* funny," Josh smiled as he tickled his daughter's side. Her limbs were flailing as she struggled to get free, but Josh kept his hold as he passed us to drop Susie on the couch.

"What did she do?" I asked.

Courtney, Josh's wife, finally made it through the threshold, attempting to hold her laughter in as she shut the door behind her, "She ran out to greet us. Josh got excited and crouched down to open his arms for a hug, and—" She covered her hand with her mouth, her eyes watering as she struggled to compose herself, "Susie turned around, bent over and—and farted—"

Logan dropped his hands from his daughter, unable to detach her from my leg yet, and covered both of his large hands with his face as he struggled through his quiet laughter. Eloise lifted her head back and cackled.

Courtney couldn't hold it in anymore and tucked her shirt over her face to laugh.

"You think it's funny to try to give me pink eye?" Josh called from the living room, attacking Susie with tickles until she was pink in the face, "How would you like it if I farted on you?" He turned around and pretended to sit on Susie. He supported enough of his weight by clutching the arm of the couch but kept her pinned beneath him.

"No! Don't do it! Yours are deadly!" Susie cried.

"It's only fair!" Josh taunted, wiggling his butt for theatrics.

In front of me, Logan finally untangled his daughter from my leg. She was now dead weight as her dad tried to get her to stand up and slip her shoes on. Iris wouldn't have it, she kept flopping onto the hardwood floor, making it as difficult for her dad as possible.

Eloise crouched down, accepting her daughter's faceplant onto the floor, and started to slide her shoes on anyway.

"Were you good for T today?" Eloise asked her daughter.

"I was perfect," Iris promptly responded with a nod against the floor.

I snorted, but backed her up, "She was great."

34

Logan helped Eloise gather their daughter's things before he tiptoed upstairs to get their sleeping baby; a car seat looped on his arm.

After that, Eloise and Logan eventually waved goodbye and piled into their truck.

Courtney and Josh were chatting with Susie, so I decided to excuse myself and call it a night.

I stepped out onto their porch, inhaling the cool, fresh nighttime air. Thick with humidity. Just how I liked it.

It was quiet on their street.

The sound of Courtney laughing and Susie's voice rambling on about something, attempting to be heard over her mother's laugh, made something ache in my chest.

Loneliness.

I winced at my own thought. Lonely? I wasn't lonely. I loved being alone. I appreciated what all my friends had, but I didn't need that myself. I didn't need the marriage and white picket fence with two-point-five kids and a dog.

It was all so...*hetero.*

I shook the thought away, annoyed with myself as I settled into my car.

Big, brown eyes and dark black hair kept filling my vision the entire drive home.

Chapter Four

TAYLOR

"Hi, Jacqueline," I approached my teammate's girlfriend casually, knowing she was the one I could get information from with little to no follow-up questions. Leo was waltzing over to us after saying goodbye to Zaid, so my time was running out.

"Hi, T," Jacqueline's dark brown eyes slid over to her boyfriend.

"Nicole didn't want to come watch us today?" I asked as I bent down to grab my water bottle. I was attempting to look casual about my inquiry.

"I didn't ask," Jacqueline lifted a shoulder with her response. Her gaze flicked over to me for a moment before focusing on her boyfriend again. I could practically see the little cartoon hearts a la *Heartstopper* floating around her head.

"Huh," I took a sip before capping my bottle, I could hear Leo's feet thumping on the grass as he picked up his pace to reach us, "Maybe I should ask her."

Jacqueline shrugged again, clearly not focused on this conversation at all.

Perfect.

"Could I get her number from you?"

Jacqueline immediately reached into her pocket and slid her phone out, before pulling up the contact in question, "I'll just send you her contact."

"Thanks."

"Whose contact are you sending to T?" Leo's voice asked from right behind me.

Dammit.

"Nicole's," Jacqueline answered immediately.

"Oh *really*?" Leo bent to kiss his girlfriend's head, before plopping himself next to her on the ground and raising his dark eyebrows at me, "And why do you want Nicole's number, T?"

I gave him a blank look as I responded, which wasn't hard to do since I had been giving Leo those looks since the first day we met, "No reason."

Leo snorted.

Jacqueline frowned as her dark brown eyes bounced between the two of us, "Wait, are you interested in Nicole?"

"I'm interested in inviting her to more of our practices," I said while avoiding eye contact.

Jacqueline nodded as a pinch in her brows formed, "To motivate you to play better?"

I blinked at her, "What?"

Leo was grinning from ear to ear, leaning back on his arms as he let his girlfriend explain herself.

"When you first invited me to practice, it was because you wanted Leo to show off and play better. You thought that if I were here, it would motivate him," Jacqueline nodded, "So, by your own logic, if you like Nicole, wouldn't inviting her here make you play better, too?"

Well.

Leave it to Jacqueline to lay it all out there like that.

Might as well admit defeat.

"What if I was interested in Nicole?" I asked my question as I plopped down next to them, crossing one ankle over the other as we enjoyed the cool breeze brushing over the grass.

"Then you should ask her out," Jacqueline nodded, "But be nice. She's fragile."

I grinned at Jacqueline, "Oh, I plan on being *very* nice." I wiggled my eyebrows and winked. Jacqueline's dark eyes widened as a blush stained her cheeks, and I chuckled to myself before Leo wrapped his arms around her and pulled her against his chest.

"Jacqueline," Leo's voice lowered as he dropped his lips to her ear, "Don't let them fluster you so easily." He trailed his fingers down her arm once, and her faint blush turned bright crimson.

Yeah, Jacqueline was still mostly straight.

Unlike her boyfriend.

"What do you mean by fragile?" I asked.

Jacqueline leaned back into Leo's embrace before replying, "She's still recovering from her breakup."

I frowned at that.

I couldn't believe grown adults were still so horrible at relationships at our age. Why anyone in their thirties would think cheating on a partner instead of saying the words, "I think we should break up," was a better option, was mind-boggling to me.

People were so selfish.

Nicole didn't deserve that.

I barely knew her, but anyone with eyeballs could see how sweet she was. How kind.

The thought of anyone getting bored or annoyed with her astounded me.

I only shared one single kiss with her, and I was already becoming obsessed.

"Right," I nodded, "I can't believe that woman cheated on her."

"It's a fucked thing to do," Leo nodded as he twirled some of Jacqueline's hair between his fingers. His eyes were focused on the lock of hair as he continued, "I think you're a good rebound for her, though."

I felt the pinch in my forehead form before I caught myself and smoothed it out.

I grinned, but it felt...off.

Rebound? Was that all I was good for?

Leo knew I wasn't interested in settling down with anyone soon, so I couldn't give his word choice too much grief. But something about the bluntness of it stung all the same.

But...*why* did it sting?

"Yeah," Jacqueline sighed, snuggling into a smelly Leo some more, "Maybe you can help get her confidence back."

I nodded before checking my phone to ensure Nicole's contact information went through to mine.

"I'm happy to help if she's interested," I shouldered my bag, and nodding to my friends, said, "I'm going to head out. See you next week." I saluted the two of them while they waved back at me.

Rebound...

I was the *rebound*.

It made sense. She had recently been in a long-term relationship, and I pretty much avoided long-term relationships simply because it never felt right to me.

I never thought too much about it before.

So why was I stuck on Leo's choice of words?

Hypothetically, let's say his words bothered me because I

didn't want to be a rebound. Hypothetically, let's say that I did want a more substantial relationship with Nicole. I was allowed to change my mind, wasn't I? I mean, it's not every day *I* find someone who makes my heart do circus tricks in my ribcage.

I shook my head before heading to my car.

This was all too soon to say.

Step one, I needed to text her.

See what her vibe was, as the youths say.

I shouldn't get ahead of myself.

Settling into the driver's seat, I pulled my phone out and tapped on her new contact information, opening a new text thread.

Chapter Five

NICOLE

"HI, NICOLE," Jacqueline's voice echoed from the hallway right as I locked my office door.

"Hi, Jacqueline," I smiled at the CHRO before both of our gazes slid over to Brandon, the CEO of Sun Steer, walking out of his office.

"Done for the day?" He asked the two of us. We both shouldered our bags, our office lights were off, and we were locking up. Just like him.

"Yup," I replied. It was only 3:00 pm, but I had done all the work I could force myself to do. It was a week after that kiss with Taylor Desmond, and I often found myself staring into space, thinking about the feel of their lips on mine. How their septum ring felt pressed against my lip and cheek.

"Are you going to be in the office tomorrow, Jacqueline?" Brandon asked as the two of us joined him. Coming from the CEO of Sun Steer, usually, that question would make someone nervous. Not here, though. It took me all of one week to understand how laid-back Brandon was. It was very different coming from my previous company, Blix.

Jacqueline worked there, too, apparently. That's how big the multi-billion-dollar company was. We never bumped into each other.

Sun Steer was growing, and I could see a future where the company grew as large as Blix, but the difference would be all because of Brandon Moore.

In a world filled with shitty CEOs and unethical billionaires, Brandon Moore was an example of what a CEO *should* be. When he founded this company with Zaid back in the day, they both had a vision for what the ethics of the company would look like. Surprisingly, Brandon has made sure they kept to it.

It was something I was shocked to see when I first stepped into my position as CFO here. A blonde-haired, straight cis white man not making grabby hands at any and all profits his company made?

Unheard of.

Upper management got paid well. I was able to live on my own in an elevated part of Orange County, just a few minutes from the Irvine offices. My HOA had multiple pools, hot tubs, a pickleball court, a yoga studio, and other amenities I hadn't even explored yet. I still lived in a relatively small one-bedroom apartment, but the fact that I could earn a livable wage on my own, and maintain a savings account in this economy, wasn't something to blink at.

During one of the first meetings I had with Brandon, regarding overall budgets for things like new hires, I noticed what the lowest-paid employee was making at Sun Steer.

It was over six figures.

When I casually brought this up with him, trying to compliment him without seeming like I was sucking up, he just shrugged and said, "If the lowest-level full-time employee at Sun Steer isn't making enough money and needs to get a second job, Sun Steer doesn't deserve to be in business. People don't go to work because they love to work, they go to work because they need to get paid to live. As a company, we've seemed to deal with less turnover by simply paying our employees enough to live close to the office."

After going over the numbers, I also learned that Brandon also made sure that upper management never made more than 4x the amount of the lowest-paid employee in the company.

I never wanted to work anywhere else.

"Yeah, I'll be here," Jacqueline replied as she popped her earbuds in, bringing me back to the present, "I'm interviewing a couple of candidates for Signe's replacement."

Signe's career as a romance author was taking off, and she was finally able to give notice that she would be quitting within a couple of months.

At my old job, if I knew someone was leaving soon, I wouldn't expect to see much of them again after they quit. However, I noticed a warm, happy feeling in my stomach when I realized that I would still hang out with Signe regularly. We had a friendship outside of work, that wouldn't end just because we didn't clock in at the same time in the same place anymore.

Signe was *my* friend. Not Colleen's. Not Sun Steer's. Mine.

A connection I made all on my own, without the help of whoever I was dating.

"Great, I wanted to meet with you both regarding catering options for the end-of-summer company party." Brandon nodded as he walked with us toward the elevators, pressing the button to call them up.

"Oh, we should cater dinner and dessert," I nodded. I *love* dessert.

"I'd like that," Jacqueline widened her eyes, before asking Brandon, "I can't remember, is this party for employees only, or are family and friends invited?"

"Family and friends are invited," Brandon nodded as he thumbed away on his phone.

"Cool," Jacqueline turned to me then, "You should invite Taylor."

I stiffened before the elevator doors opened, "What?"

Jacqueline stepped through as Brandon gestured for me to follow behind her.

"You should invite Taylor," Jacqueline repeated. She spoke a little more clearly as if my question was because I didn't hear her the first time.

I nodded, "Oh. Why?"

Jacqueline looked at me, before glancing at my phone in my hands, "Because—wait, didn't they text you?"

I widened my eyes, "Were they going to text me?"

Jacqueline frowned before her eyes widened and her lips parted, "Oh. Maybe I wasn't supposed to say anything." Ever since Jacqueline got her autism diagnosis, she has been less worried about masking around everyone and more comfortable explaining herself with words that made the most sense to her. A couple of weeks after confessing her love to Leo at his rugby practice, she decided to "pull the trigger" and get formally tested. I remembered being with Jacqueline at a girls' night with all of us, including Mary and Jamie (who also worked at Sun Steer), while her phone rang with the incoming call.

When Jacqueline's autism diagnosis was confirmed, she cried.

Then we all started crying with her, hugging her and

congratulating her on finally having the answers she'd been wondering about her whole life.

"No, actually," I lifted a finger, "I think you should say something. More things. Did they tell you they were going to call me?"

Jacqueline pressed her lips together, glancing at Brandon, who seemed mildly amused with the conversation as the elevator started its descent.

"They just asked me for your number," Jacqueline said, staying perfectly still as she replied.

"Why?" I pressed.

Jacqueline squinted her eyes as she faced forward, avoiding my gaze, "I really don't know if I should say."

"Jacqueline," I reached forward and squeezed her bicep, "I want to know why someone wanted my contact information." I raised my eyebrows at her, and she nodded once before exhaling and replying.

"They said they were interested in asking you out."

A swarm of butterflies took off in my stomach from her words, "Really?" I noticed right then that I was smiling, and I removed my hand from Jacqueline's bicep to press my hand to my cheek.

Yup. I was blushing.

"Oh. I see," I tried to keep my cool, but I couldn't.

Taylor was *interested* in me.

I was a grown woman, closer to forty years old than thirty, and yet I was still blushing as if I were a teenager who had just discovered her first crush.

Then, as my stomach dropped, I realized something.

"They haven't texted me yet," I sighed the words when the elevator doors opened, and we all filed off the elevator.

"They will," Jacqueline nodded to herself, "They were

blushing like you are when they asked me for your number."

"Should I—" I stopped, letting Brandon walk ahead a bit as Jacqueline loitered in the lobby with me, "I mean, do you think—if they text me—that I should go out with them?"

Jacqueline shrugged, "If you want to."

I did want to, but that didn't necessarily mean I *should*.

Her dark eyes studied me in that intense way that intimidated more people than not. Before I could continue, Jacqueline spoke up again.

"Taylor is one of my favorite people. I think you'd have fun with them." She nodded to herself, as if settling the discussion.

Perhaps it really was as simple as that.

"Yeah. I think you're right," I murmured.

And with that, Jacqueline smiled and pulled her phone out, waving goodbye before we parted ways.

I stood there in the lobby of our building for a moment, staring at Jacqueline's retreating form, while trying to picture Taylor Desmond blushing while asking for my phone number.

I couldn't.

Did they even get nervous? I wouldn't peg them as someone who got nervous asking for someone's number.

I replayed that conversation with Jacqueline multiple times in my head on the drive home. Trying to remember every detail, wondering if I heard Jacqueline right or if I made the entire conversation up in my head.

Was I ready to date someone like Taylor?

Did they even want to date, or did they just want to hook up?

I remembered Sarah's words from the previous week, how Taylor didn't "do relationships."

46

I frowned to myself.

But...maybe I needed a break from relationships too.

Maybe I needed to have fun with someone like Taylor, to help me get my groove back.

I didn't realize how thrilling the idea sounded to me until later, when I was fixing myself some dinner and heard my phone vibrate on my kitchen countertop.

An unknown number had just texted me.

I stopped what I was doing to swipe at the notification with trembling fingers.

Hey, it's Taylor.

Chapter Six

TAXLOR

Me: Hey, it's Taylor.

Me: I got your number from Jacqueline. I hope that's okay.

Nicole: Hi! That's okay (:

I DRUMMED my hands on the legs of my jeans, wondering how best to respond.

I never continued the conversation last night. Nerves coated my veins, and part of me was still struggling to figure out *what* exactly I wanted from this exchange.

"Hi T," Violet Thompson's voice echoed through my office, so I was already smiling by the time I turned around in my chair to greet her and little Gracie.

"Hi!" I jumped up from my chair, collecting Gracie's favorite items from the cabinet while she and her mom settled around the little table in the center of the room. "Are you all packed and ready to go?"

"Almost," Violet sighed as she watched her daughter dig

her hands into her favorite sensory bin. Beans and rice, with little marbles for her to collect if she so desired. Gracie's eyes lit up as soon as her little hands disappeared into the bin, so I took my time thinking about what I wanted to work on with her today.

"What else do you have to pack?" I asked.

"Just Gracie's room. And the bathroom," Violet sighed as she pulled her electric blue hair out of her ponytail and started to braid it, her green eyes on her daughter to ensure the little stinker didn't shove any dried beans into her mouth, "The kitchen—oh, and my bedroom, I guess—"

"Don't you live in a two-bedroom apartment?" I chuckled as I set my items on the table in front of Gracie and her mom before I took my own seat next to them, "Isn't that just your whole apartment, then?"

"I guess one could argue that I haven't started packing yet," Violet gave me a sly smile as she slowly trailed her fingers in the sensory bin with her daughter, "But my dad has."

"Good on Frank," I smiled. I had only met her dad a couple of times over the years, but the man was a silver fox.

"He's very excited," Violet nodded. "Anyway, what do you have planned for us today?"

"I was thinking—" my phone buzzed on the tabletop. I became distracted as soon as I saw Nicole's contact show up on it. I snatched the device in my hands, swiping the notification without thought.

> Nicole: I just wanted to thank you for helping me deal with my ex the other day. You didn't have to do that, but I appreciate it.

I stared at her message, wondering how to use this to keep the conversation going.

"Who's that?" Violet asked over her daughter's blonde head. I jerked my gaze up from my phone to see her not-so-subtly peering to look at my phone screen.

"It's Nic—" I cut myself off. Nicole was Violet's superior. She worked at the same company as Leo and Jacqueline. Was this what it was like dating in your late thirties? Everyone knowing everyone?

"Nick?" Violet asked.

I stared at her for another moment.

To tell her, or not to tell her?

I shook my head; I was a grown adult.

"It's Nicole," I cleared my throat as heat stained my cheeks from the admission. *Fuck.* I never blushed like this.

"Oh," Violet nodded, "...Wait, like *my* Nicole?"

I caught myself before I frowned.

I didn't like the sound of that.

I knew what Violet meant, I knew that Violet was, as far as I could tell, mostly straight. That she and Nicole weren't like that. But that didn't mean I liked hearing her say those words. *My Nicole.*

Nicole didn't belong to anyone.

Not her ex.

Not Violet.

Frankly, not even me.

Which, weirdly, didn't make me feel better.

"Yeah," I shrugged as I watched Violet and Gracie play in the sensory bin together.

"You two text each other?"

"Now we do," I plucked a marble out of the sensory bin and gently set it on the table, watching as Gracie frowned and snatched the marble with her little fingers, before placing it back in the bin with the rest of them. I smiled at the little girl, loving how her brain worked.

Violet opened her mouth to respond, but I was saved from having to explain *why* I was texting another coworker of hers by one of mine gently knocking on the door and entering my office.

Beck's hazel eyes and dark brown hair greeted us as she said, "Hi, sorry to interrupt."

"You're fine," I smiled at my long-time friend, "What's up?"

"I'm just delivering this," Beck quietly stepped into the room to set a hot coffee on my desk, careful not to startle Gracie or throw off her routine. "Also, we're going to visit Gram later if you want to join us."

I gave her a thumbs up, "I'll be there."

"Sounds good," Beck turned to Violet, "You're getting ready to move soon, yeah?"

"Yeah," Violet sighed, "I have lots of feelings about it." She gently tucked a blonde curl out of her daughter's face, who hummed as she focused on her sensory bin.

"Post lots of pictures," Beck replied with a grin, "It's *so* beautiful up there. I love how green northern California is."

"You're so right," Violet grinned back, but she looked nervous. "I will. Say bye, Gracie." Violet prompted her daughter by tapping her on the shoulder. Gracie glanced up at Beck, her former speech therapist, and stared for a solid three seconds before focusing back on her bin.

"Take care, Gracie!" Beck signed her goodbye as well, before ducking out of the room.

"Who is Gram?" Violet immediately asked.

I smiled, a familiar but faded ache burning in my chest at the question.

"Beck's grandmother," I replied, "She passed away a few years ago. We visit her grave every now and then."

Susan Scott was an icon. Both sets of my grandparents

had passed away when I was too young to build any memories with them. My older brother had memories and told me stories about my grandparents, but I always felt left out. When I became friends with Beck after starting work here at the clinic, she was living with her grandmother at the time. After many movie and game nights at the townhouse that Courtney and Josh now resided in, Susan Scott became an honorary grandparent of mine. She considered all of us her honorary grandchildren.

For the longest time, she and I were the only openly queer people in our little trusted circle of friendship—until Courtney reconnected with Josh at one of his concerts. Because of this, I felt like she and I had a special understanding of each other. How many people my age could say that they had a queer grandparent they could look up to? Susan Scott wasn't my grandmother by blood, but she was my Gram in all the ways that truly mattered.

"That's sweet," Violet replied, seconds before Gracie grabbed a handful of beans and tossed them across the room. "Girl, why?"

I smirked. Violet was a hilarious mom. Not only was she shamelessly alt with her tattoos and bright blue hair, but she also spoke to her daughter as an equal.

Gracie ignored her mom and dug her fist in the beans again, grabbing a large handful, before Violet grasped her daughter's wrist to keep her from chucking the contents of the sensory bin again.

"No, thank you," Violet signed the word *no* for Gracie with her free hand, just like Beck taught her to. "We're going to be all done with the bin if you toss it again."

With that, we settled into the routine of the session. Reeling little Gracie in and working on fun activities to help strengthen her fine motor skills. We weren't entirely sure what her care would look like up in northern California since it was significantly less populated and therefore had fewer resources to offer neurodivergent children, but I assured Violet at the end of our session that I'm no more than a call or text away if she needed help.

After Violet pulled me in for a hug, she thanked me one last time.

"Of course, I'm going to miss you all," I crouched down to Gracie's level, holding my palm up, "Have so much fun on your new adventure, little Gracie." Gracie smiled at me and gave me a high-five before holding her mom's hand and being led out of the office.

I had a few hours before my next client, due to last-minute cancelations, so I decided to make the most of my free time by catching up on some paperwork.

Then I decided not to do that at all and found myself staring at Nicole's message with my hands running through my hair.

This was exactly how Courtney and Beck found me later when it was time to eat lunch in the break room.

"I don't think I've ever seen you hunched over your desk like that, ever," Courtney's words startled me out of my spiral because I hadn't realized that they entered my office until she spoke, "What's up, T?"

I spun in my chair, inhaling through my nose when the aroma of pasta filled the space.

"Did he make enough for me?" I asked, crossing both of my fingers at her.

Courtney smiled, "Of course, and probably enough for leftovers, too." She and Beck both lifted large bags. Courtney and Josh had a professional chef at home that kept their refrigerator stocked with prepared meals at all times. They started using him after Susie was born, to help them through Courtney's postpartum. But Josh was loaded, as world-famous rock stars usually were, so they kept him on.

Once you hire a private chef who handles all meal planning for you, it's difficult to go back.

Courtney didn't work at the clinic anymore, choosing to become a full-time mommy to little Susie and Cooper, instead. However, she still brought lunches for Beck, Beck's boyfriend, and me.

"Hell yeah, brother," I stood from my chair and took a step toward them, before remembering my phone and snatching it off the desk to shove into my pocket.

"What are you stressed about?" Beck asked as the three of us made it over to the break room of the clinic.

"Who says I'm stressed?" I replied.

"The hunch in your shoulders," Courtney replied, resting her hand on the said shoulder and gently pushing down so it wasn't hunched near my head. Frick.

I sighed, before pulling my phone out of my pocket.

These were the women I wanted to talk to about this.

"I'm wondering how to respond to these texts," I pulled up the conversation with Nicole as we entered the breakroom. Beck grabbed my phone and studied the exchange as all three of us pulled seats out and settled in.

As Beck passed the phone to Courtney to look at, Beck's boyfriend silently entered the break room and started divvying out lunch for all of us.

We'd come a long way from sack lunches and snack packs.

"Hi Adam," I held my fist out for him to bump.

"Hey," He replied. As soon as he dished everyone their meals and sat next to Beck, Courtney spoke up.

"I'm confused, you started this conversation," Courtney handed my phone back to me.

"I did," I sighed, twirling my pasta around on my fork, "But I'm feeling nervous."

"Why?" Beck asked around a mouthful of food.

I leaned back in my chair, quirking my lips to the side in thought.

"This woman is really fucking pretty," I admitted, "We kissed the other day to make her ex jealous, and it's all I can think about now."

Beck wiggled her eyebrows, whereas Courtney rubbed her hands together as if she were a villain planning something.

"It was a good kiss, then?" Courtney clarified.

"*So* good," I pressed my lips together, "I'm just not entirely sure she wants more."

"I think she does," Beck nodded toward my phone, now resting on the table. "She sent a double text. And a smiley face."

I nodded, scratching the back of my head. I usually kept it short and sometimes went the extra mile to shave little designs in the short hair. But I'd been letting it grow out a bit more. I could run my fingers through it. I could grip my hair near my neck, and I couldn't remember the last time I could do that.

"God, I'm being ridiculous," I dropped my utensil to scrape both of my hands down my face, shaking my head as I picked my phone up, "I'm going to respond."

"Do it," Beck encouraged with a nod of her head.

Me: No problem.

I sent that, and then immediately groaned. I pushed my

plate out of the way so I could drop my head to the table appropriately, considering how humiliating my texting game was at the moment.

"No problem? T, what the hell is wrong with you?" Courtney asked after looking at my phone, "Just tell her you want to kiss her again."

"Yeah," I lifted my head, staring wide-eyed at Courtney, "Good idea." I must have looked insane because Courtney's brows rose as she subtly leaned away from me in her seat. She threw Beck a look, but I focused on my phone as I sent my own double text.

I was going to send what Courtney suggested word for word, but I thought about it for two more seconds and decided to go a flirtier route, just in case she wanted to gently turn me down.

> Me: If you need me to scare off any more of your exes, I'm only a text away now.

There. That felt a little better.

God, this woman.

Courtney snorted next to me, indicating that she read what I sent over my shoulder.

I set my phone down and focused on taking bites of food. Desperate not to spiral and wait for those dancing three dots to show up at the bottom of the screen.

Nicole was a CFO.

She was probably very busy.

She probably wouldn't see that text until later—

Bzzzz.

"What'd she say?" Beck asked, leaning toward me from the other side of the table.

My phone was already in my hands, my eyes reading her text as fast as possible.

Nicole: What do you mean by that?

I sighed, rubbing the back of my neck with my hand before thumbing a response. I needed to rip the band-aid off here. I needed to let her know I was interested. Very interested. If she wasn't, she could put me out of my misery. I could redownload any of the dozens of dating apps I had and find someone else to hyper-fixate on.

Even though I'd never been hyper-fixated on anyone before.

Not even when I was in a committed relationship.

What I was experiencing now was new territory for me.

Me: I mean, I really enjoyed scaring off your ex. So, if you ever needed to again, we could even practice scaring off our ex in the future—you know, to get it *just* right. Or you can tell me to fuck off, and I will. Your call, babe.

I set the phone down, feeling more like myself.

"This is crazy," I murmured to myself. The table was silent, which made me glance up to see all three of my friends studying me with a myriad of expressions.

Adam's face almost looked bored, which was normal for him. However, I noticed that one eyebrow was slightly raised as he studied me. Beck's eyes were wide; she had a mouthful of food she had paused chewing as she stared at me. Courtney's lips were parted as she furrowed her brows at me.

"You're acting so weird," Courtney said with a shake of her head, "You're never this nervous about texting people."

"I know, I don't know what's wrong with me." I rested my hand on my chest, "My heart is racing like a mile a minute."

"Huh," Beck hummed to herself after swallowing her bite, "I remember feeling like that about Adam." She took another bite and chewed thoughtfully before adding, "It's important to keep in mind that I have an anxiety disorder, though."

Adam leaned over to kiss the crown of her head before focusing back on his meal.

"I think you were just *really* into me," Adam murmured.

"Were?" Beck asked with a grin.

Courtney and I both shared a look and pretended to choke back vomit.

"Over a decade later, and you're still gross and in love," I shook my head, "Though I am wondering if I'm just *really* into Nicole."

"That's exciting," Courtney wiggled her eyebrows now as she added, "The butterflies in the stomach stages are the most fun."

"I don't usually *get* butterflies," I replied, "I'm known to *give* butterflies, though."

"Maybe Nicole is different," Beck lifted a shoulder with her words, "Maybe—oh my god she responded." She cut herself off when my phone buzzed on the table again.

I kept the phone on the table but swiped the notification so all three of us could read her message.

> Nicole: Hmm. What kinds of things should we practice on? To get things "just right," as you said.

"Alright," I snatched my phone off the table, out of their sight, "That ends your friend privileges."

Beck and Courtney both whined at that, pretending to be put out by no longer being allowed to read my texts with Nicole.

Also, *holy shit, Nicole was playing along!*

"Why were your privileges revoked?" Adam asked since he wasn't leaning on the table to read off my phone.

What would be sexy to respond with, but not too sexy?

"It was getting a little heated," Beck explained, "To the point where Nicole might start sending messages she didn't consent to others reading."

"Ah," Adam nodded, then furrowed his brows, "...You don't show spicy text messages to each other?"

God, I couldn't wait to feel Nicole's lips on mine again.

"Oh, we do," Courtney clarified, "But the circumstances need to be justified."

"Exactly," Beck responded, "If you want a second opinion on how to interpret the text message. Or if you're asking for advice on how to respond to keep it going. Or, obviously, if you're feeling unsafe."

"But in T's case," Courtney jutted a thumb toward me, "They never need advice on how to sext someone. Or how to interpret a spicy text. Therefore, there's no good reason for Beck and me to read all the filthy things they're about to start sending Nicole. That's private between the two of them."

"Ah," Adam nodded his head, "I was under the impression that you three just shared everything, but I guess these boundaries make sense."

"Beck has shared more than enough," I replied as I held my phone in my hands, still brainstorming my response to Nicole, "But also," I winked at Adam, just to make him uncomfortable, "You're a dirty dog."

Adam didn't act uncomfortable, because he's known me for over a decade now and was used to me trying to rile people up for the thrill of it. Instead, he just nodded and said, "Thanks."

Beck giggled.

"I strive to be as unbothered as Adam Hall." Courtney sighed to herself, "If Josh were here, he'd demand a whole detailed analysis of his spicy texting over the years."

"I can see him shoving his glasses up his nose and clicking his pen before taking notes," I snickered.

Finally, I responded.

> Me: Well, you don't need to practice kissing. You have that down to an art. However, if you wanted to "practice sleeping with someone who isn't a cheater," I am happy to volunteer for the job.

The conversation shifted during the rest of the lunch hour, more focused on the plans for visiting Susan's grave. I was remembering Jacqueline's words, how Nicole was fragile. She was still recovering from her shitty breakup. I didn't want to push her; I wanted everything that happened between the two of us to be entirely consensual.

But when my phone buzzed one more time, I felt a thrill of heat warm my veins at her response.

> Nicole: Well, for the sake of "practice," I think I might take you up on that (:

FALLING FOR TIME

Chapter Seven
NICOLE

I sat there staring at the last exchange we had, stepping off the elevator and making my way toward the parking lot.

> Taylor: Are you busy tonight?

> Me: Not at all. Want to come over?

> Taylor: Yes. Address?

I was going to have a hook-up. I was going to hook up with Taylor Desmond. We weren't even going to go on a date. They were just going to come over and we'd mash our mouths together again.

Probably.

Hopefully.

My heart was beating in my chest, excitement making me twitchy as I made it home and watched the time go by. Getting closer and closer to the time we agreed on.

It's real, Nicole. You're really doing this.

I was both nervous and excited. I was desperately trying not to think too much about this.

When a knock sounded on my door, I jumped in my seat. I practically fell off the barstool as I rounded the kitchen counter to answer.

When I opened my front door, I felt surprised to see them there. Which was ridiculous. I invited them over. I expected to see them there. And yet, staring at Taylor on the threshold of my apartment felt almost *too* real.

They wore their jeans low on their waist. I could see the protrusion of their hip bones peaking underneath their cropped t-shirt. A dramatic divot parted their abdominal muscles.

"How old are you?" I asked before licking my lips. God, what a stupid thing to ask. I waved them in, and they stepped through to allow me to shut the front door.

My throat was suddenly so dry. I swallowed around nothing. My heart was pounding at a rate that couldn't be sustainable.

They lifted a dark brow at me from my question, before their pink lips parted in a sly smile, "Thirty-nine."

I widened my eyes. "What?" That was very unexpected.

Taylor widened their eyes, too, clearly mocking my reaction.

"Is that a problem?"

"I assumed I was older than you." Instead, they were two years older than *me*, "What's your skincare routine?"

Taylor smirked, and a lighthearted laugh escaped their lips. From the way their shoulders relaxed, I could have sworn they looked relieved. "It's not easy maintaining skin as soft and touchable as mine."

My fingers twitched at my sides as if to feel for myself.

Taylor clocked the movement, and their dark blue eyes danced with amusement.

"...We need to address this." Taylor nodded to

themselves with their words. Their gaze lowered, and my skin burned where it landed. Trailing over my body, taking in everything. I wasn't even wearing anything that seductive, but the way Taylor Desmond studied me, I felt like the sexiest woman alive.

"Address what?" I asked.

"This," They lifted a finger to gesture between us as they took a step toward me, "Because I don't know if I'm capable of small talk when you're standing there, all nervous and blushing and mouthwatering."

I swallowed around nothing, before replying, "Y-you can't?"

"No," Taylor shook their head, and the visual of them darting their tongue out to moisten their bottom lip made something throb in my core. "What about you?"

Breathe, Nicole. Breathe.

Maintaining eye contact, I slowly, slowly shook my head in the negative.

Taylor exhaled with a nod of their head. They pressed their lips together as their gaze danced across my face, probably noticing how flushed mine was. Only a couple of inches separated us now.

How did they get so close?

How did they smell so fucking good?

I swayed toward them, leaning into it with a tentative step.

Less than an inch separated our chests now.

"So, let's skip the small talk," and then, without warning, they cupped my jaw and captured my lips with theirs.

My heart stopped.

And then kickstarted all over again.

Blood was rushing in my ears from the thrill of kissing Taylor Desmond again. It wasn't like our first kiss. The show we put on in the bar to get rid of my ex. No, this was heated and heavy. I swiped my tongue across their lips, and they opened so I could tangle my tongue with theirs with greed.

Because their hands still cupped my jaw, I wrapped my arms under theirs, digging my nails into their smooth back so we could be pressed together completely.

Their harder body molded with my soft, and I moaned when they stepped a thigh between my legs. I could feel their hardened nipples scrape against my fuller breasts, and I shivered.

"God, I needed this," they murmured against my lips before licking into my mouth again, "You're so sweet."

I whimpered at their praise, shifting my hips against their thigh in a way I was *hoping* felt sexy and not completely desperate.

They tugged on my bottom lip with their teeth, and I happily followed their retreat. I couldn't remember the last time a person turned me on this much. Taylor's hands were suddenly all over me. One cupped the back of my head while the other found my hip, sliding their fingers underneath the hem of my shirt.

Their fingertips danced across my skin for a moment before they released my lips, smirking as I gasped for air, "Can I...?" Their fingers trailed up my ribcage just a hair. Their dark blue eyes were almost entirely concealed by their black pupils.

"Yes," I breathed my response.

Taylor sighed before capturing my mouth again, dragging their hand up to boldly palm my breast. They gently squeezed, and when my lips parted in a gasp, they licked into my mouth again.

I was being completely consumed by Taylor Desmond, and I had never felt more alive.

"Gorgeous," Taylor murmured against my lips. They finally let up, allowing me to catch my breath as their warm lips trailed, dragging kisses across my jaw, over to my ear, "Do you have any idea how often I've daydreamed about playing with your perfect tits since our kiss?"

I smiled, flattered. Both of their hands started to paw my bra cups down, allowing their thumbs to brush over my nipples.

"Can I touch you back?" I asked. My voice sounded breathless and sultry, and I blushed again at how turned on I was. I ground my hips against their leg, gasping at the warm friction developing between my legs.

"Please," Taylor nipped at my ear before reaching behind themselves to grab one of my wrists. My pulse raced so hard under their touch that I was sure they could feel it. As they teased my neck with their lips, they slowly slid my hand underneath their shirt.

I dragged my knuckles against their stomach, so flat and firm.

They were athletic and fit. Strong. As I dragged my hand higher, I wasn't too surprised to see that they weren't wearing a bra of their own.

They didn't need to. Their breasts were much, much smaller than mine. But when I brushed my fingertips over their chest, they shuddered.

"Are you..." I swallowed. "Are you wet for me, too?"

Taylor chuckled against my neck. They pressed themselves against my body more, pinning me against the wall as they rubbed against my thigh. We each had a leg between the other, and I moaned from the friction their thrusts created for me.

"I'm fucking soaked, Nicole," Taylor groaned in my ear, "Every time I see you, I'm soaked."

I leaned back, trailing my hands down their chest so that I could start undoing the button on their jeans. "I want to feel you."

Taylor chuckled before leaning back and tugging my shorts down, too. "I might need to feel you first." Their eyes were deliciously hooded. Their cheeks were beautifully flushed. When I noted their swollen lips from our kisses, another rush of arousal flooded my system.

I giggled before shoving their jeans down, revealing low-hung boxers underneath. I grinned up at them when I realized there was an open flap in the front.

"This is convenient," I smirked as I traced a finger against them. I could feel a tuft of curls, but then their hips flexed against my hand, and just like that, my fingers were brushing against their damp core.

"Fuck, Nicole," Taylor leaned forward, slapping a hand on the wall near my head, "That feels so good." I grinned. Not to toot my own horn, but I was phenomenal at fingering. It was a badge of pride I loved showing off as much as I was able to. As I positioned my hand to tease their entrance while brushing my thumb against their clit, I heard Taylor whimper near my ear.

"You're so sexy, Taylor." I turned toward their ear to whisper the words, before dragging my teeth against their lobe, "I want to watch you come undone."

"Stay tuned," Taylor sighed as their hips flexed against my hand. They were using both of their hands to support themselves against the wall now. I loved doing this to them. I loved being the one to drive Taylor to the edge like this. So quickly, too. Every time I brushed their clit just the right way, a new wave of wetness coated my fingers.

"Can I feel inside of you?" I asked them against their ear.

They managed to nod in response.

I inserted one finger, slowly, teasingly, into their core while still brushing my thumb against the most sensitive part of them.

"Oh," Taylor almost buckled at the contact, and I released a huff of amusement. I felt powerful. I felt desired. In control.

Things I hadn't felt since before Colleen.

"Almost there, babe." I licked their ear, then dragged my lips to the sensitive spot just below it and sucked.

They started pulsing around my fingers, clenching hard as they groaned through their orgasm. My hand was drenched as I continued to work their clit, over and over again. Their orgasm just kept going, and I felt like I was on cloud nine watching them come undone against me.

Finally, they gasped and wrapped one of their hands around my wrist, "Oh my god." They breathed.

I grinned, taking in their post-orgasmic glow brightening their cheeks.

Suddenly, they pecked me on the nose and dropped to their knees.

"Oh—"

"Your turn, beautiful." Taylor grinned as they roughly yanked my shorts down. "I need to taste you." I blushed, hard. I didn't usually engage in oral the first time I was with someone. Instead, my past girlfriends and I focused on kissing and hand stuff. We worked our way up, usually because I was the one who wanted to wait. But the sight of Taylor on their knees in front of me, helping me step out of my shorts, I knew I would break my rule.

"These are fucking adorable," Taylor murmured before tugging my lacy panties down and off my feet, "God, you're too much for me, Nicole." They glanced up at me, winking.

A sparkle in their eye before they grabbed one of my legs and lifted it over their slender shoulder.

"I'm—I'm sorry?" I stammered. Taylor laughed before giving me a wicked smirk and delving into me, tongue first.

I immediately slapped my hand over my mouth, muffling my cry as they dragged their tongue through my wet center. Tasting everything. It was so intimate, so thorough. I usually needed *way* more teasing than this. But somehow, Taylor feasted on me in a way that was about to get me off in less than two minutes.

They hummed as they wrapped their lips around my clit, sucking.

Just like that, I came, and it was the fastest I had ever done so.

I throbbed around their face, gasping through the electricity coursing through my veins. Pulses of pleasure pounded through my core. My muscles in my body locked, leaving Taylor to support my body while riding out my orgasm for as long I could handle it.

I used my free hand to tangle my fingers in the roots of their hair, desperate to make it last.

"That's it," Taylor murmured against my pussy, "Ride my face, babe."

We had both referred to each other as our fake pet name, and a thrill of excitement rushed in my veins from the realization. Is this what it would be like to be with Taylor? To have their partnership? Their intimacy?

I eventually came down from the high of orgasm, sagging against the wall while Taylor untucked my thigh from their shoulder. They glanced up at me as they wiped the back of their hand over their mouth, and another blush scorched my cheeks.

They stood tall, their chest heaving as we made unwavering eye contact.

"...Hi," I whispered.

Taylor bit their lip before giving me a teasing smirk and replying, "Hi."

Then, they kissed me.

I could taste myself on their lips, and a new flame burned in my chest from the arousal flooding my system.

I wanted *more*.

Silently, I laced their fingers with mine and led them to my bedroom. It was girly and feminine and covered with florals and pastels. I loved it. It was me.

When Taylor smiled after taking a quick glance at everything, I felt more relaxed.

It was crazy, how a simple smile of approval from them gave me a drop of confidence. How that confidence stayed with me when we tumbled onto the bed together. When we kept kissing and touching each other.

Even when a couple of hours passed, and my body couldn't physically orgasm again if I wanted to.

Taylor's fingers gently traced my sensitive clit, and I ended up whimpering and rolling away from them, tucking my legs into myself. They laughed, wrapping an arm around my naked body and pulling me against their equally naked chest.

"Are you satisfied?" Taylor asked into my hair, which was probably a mess now.

"I can't see straight," I replied, murmuring into my pillow. Satisfied was an understatement.

"Can you see gay?" Taylor quipped.

I snorted, rolling over to look at them over my shoulder, "Oh my god." I laughed.

Taylor smiled, unashamed of their dad joke, and pecked

my head once more. Then they sat up and swung their legs over the side of the bed.

I nervously cleared my throat. I wasn't a hook-up person. I never engaged in a good old-fashioned fuck n' release. But that was what Taylor wanted, right? Sarah had implied that they were only into casual flings. And yet, here they were. In my apartment. I now had the memory of their dark blue eyes dancing across my face in a way that made butterflies erupt in my stomach. The romantic in me hoped that they wanted so much more.

But I was done being hopeful.

For now, at least.

"Thank you." I decided to start with sitting up as well. They had grabbed some of the aftercare wipes I liked to use and reached toward me. I reached for the wipes in their hands, cleaning myself up.

Taylor hesitated for a moment when I took the wipes from their hand, and part of me wanted to ask what was wrong, but then they quickly recovered and continued to clean themselves, too.

With a shake of their head, they said, "You don't need to thank me. I got just as much out of this as you did."

I nodded.

"Right. Sorry. I don't know, um..." I waved my hand between us. "I'm not sure what's next."

Taylor quirked their lips to the side, raising a dark eyebrow at me as they tossed their used wipes in the bin in the far corner of my room. "What do you mean?"

"Hooking up like this." I lifted a shoulder, heat scorching my skin under their intense gaze, "I don't know the protocol."

Something flickered behind their eyes, and part of me panicked that they were disappointed in my words. But the look was gone as soon as I clocked it, and then they were giving me an easy-going smile again.

"Ah." They nodded once. "Well, aftercare is always important. Are you hungry? Want to watch TV?"

I wanted to say yes. But I knew myself. If I hung out with Taylor after they gave me multiple earth-shattering orgasms, I would grow feelings. Big, intense feelings. Feelings that they probably had no intention of reciprocating. They were almost in their forties. They knew what they wanted at this point in their life.

If I couldn't convince Colleen to be mine forever, I sure as hell wouldn't be able to convince someone like Taylor.

"Actually, um," I drummed my fingers on my biceps, shifting uncomfortably in my bed, "I kind of have some work to do..."

God, why was this so awkward?

Taylor's face relaxed a bit at that. Their eyebrows raised, and their easy-going smile faltered, "Oh. Right. I'm sorry. I guess I just kind of barged in here, and..." They let their gaze rake over me before clearing their throat and glancing toward my bedroom door.

Our clothes were still out in my entryway.

A quiet laugh escaped my lips as they quickly jogged out of the room and returned with our clothes bundled in their arms.

"I'm not complaining." I didn't want them to feel like I was inconvenienced in any way. All of this was entirely consensual, "I didn't mind you barging into my apartment like this."

"You sure?" Taylor asked. They set my clothes on the bed and slowly slid their boxers up their legs. I found myself hypnotized by watching their strong and lean body slowly become hidden from view.

"Oh yeah." I grinned as I watched them get dressed, and the muscles in my face felt less stiff as time marched on. Taylor didn't seem too offended or weirded out so far. This was good.

They nodded before stepping away and glancing around my room. At that, I jumped out of bed and quickly threw a robe over myself.

"I'll walk you out," I said. I probably didn't need to announce that, but my mind was still somewhat numb from coming so many times, and I felt like I needed to narrate my actions.

In response, Taylor quietly followed me out of my room and to my front door.

"Would you..." Taylor cleared their throat with their hand on the doorknob, and pink colored the tops of their cheeks and nose, "Can I call you?"

I blinked at them, mildly surprised at their question, before I nodded, "Yeah. You can call me."

I mean, casual hook-ups with the same person could happen more than once, right?

They nodded too, shoving their hands into their jeans pockets.

"Okay. Cool. I'll see you later, then."

"See ya," I smiled as they turned the handle. I found myself watching how they reached up to adjust their septum piercing before hesitating in the threshold.

Their eyes were locked on me.

Well, my lips, actually.

"Um," Taylor's cheeks flushed again, "Can I...?" They raised a hand toward my face, their gaze bouncing between my eyes and my mouth. Shit. Kissing was so *romantic*. It was one of my favorite pastimes.

...But I probably wouldn't fall in love with Taylor over *one* goodbye kiss.

A peck.

"Yeah," I nodded, stepping closer to them to emphasize my consent.

They sighed before cupping my jaw and guiding my mouth to theirs. They were a couple of inches taller than me, but they stepped so close to my body that our chests brushed together, and my head was practically tipped back at a ninety-degree angle.

It wasn't a peck, either.

Taylor brushed their lips over mine, lingering. Then, they began nipping at my lips, tasting and tugging. I was getting dizzy; the scrape of their hand on my face made excited, nervous feelings erupt in my stomach again. Eventually, I parted my lips for them. Desperate to taste them more, to taste myself that lingered.

Before the goodbye kiss turned into a full-fledged make-out, they gently pulled back. Their nose brushed mine, and I thought I felt them shiver before detaching their body from me.

Taylor stepped back abruptly, before saluting me with a friendly grin and disappearing into the hallway of my apartment building.

I stood there, both frozen and warm from that kiss, before I finally closed the front door and sagged against it.

Shit.

I was out of my league here.

I couldn't handle being with someone like them.

I definitely shouldn't hook up with Taylor Desmond again.

Chapter Eight

THE NEXT NIGHT, I knocked on Signe Lange's apartment door before the heavy thud of her steps echoed on the other side. A moment later, she swung her door open, smiling widely.

I looked up at her, returning her smile and thankful to step into the safe space that was her studio apartment. She reached down to hug me immediately, and I reached up to reciprocate. Signe was a tall woman, almost six feet tall if I remember correctly. Probably taller than Taylor.

Don't think about them.

Right. Girls' night.

After Signe released me, she stepped aside so I could enter her space.

This was the last girls' night the women of the office were having before Violet Thompson moved about twelve hours north, starting her new position working on Moore Farms and overseeing the launch of the first solar-powered, self-driving tractors. The blue-haired systems engineer was already perched on the floor of Signe's living room/bedroom.

74

Air mattresses, blankets, pillows, and snacks were already gathered around.

I'm part of this, I reminded myself, *these women can be my people.*

"Are you all packed and ready to go?" I asked Violet, plopping down to take a seat next to her.

"Nope, but we're getting there," Violet shrugged. "We leave in just a couple of days, but we live in a small unit, so it won't take too long."

I nodded. Violet had been anxious for the last few months about forcing her daughter to move across the state and into a new home. A new life. Even though Violet's contract only said she needed to stay on-site for about a year.

"And your dad is still excited to go with you?" I pressed.

"Yeah," She grinned, "He's watched a lot of *Yellowstone*, so I think he's excited to fulfill his small-town fantasy."

I laughed when another knock sounded on Signe's door.

Mary and Jamie walked into the apartment, hand in hand, before settling in on the mass of pillows and blankets, too.

"Jacqueline's here too," Jamie giggled.

"She just hasn't detached herself from Leo's face yet." Mary rolled her eyes. She was thrilled for Jacqueline and her cousin but often pretended to be completely grossed out by the idea.

"Okay, hopefully she hurries because—what the hell?" Signe was walking toward all of us with a fresh bag of Oreos when she suddenly stopped, "Is that—oh my god—"

I glanced down at where Signe's eyes were staring wide and unblinking, but all I saw was Mary lifting a finger to her lips. She gave Signe a pleading look before saying, "Wait until Jacqueline is here."

Signe's mouth was hanging open, then snapped closed. An excited squeal sounded behind her tight lips before she plopped down next to Jamie.

Another knock sounded on her front door, and after Signe called out a message saying it was unlocked, Jacqueline finally joined the group.

Everyone was here.

"Before we get started," Signe gestured to the TV, where the movie *My Old Ass* was ready to play, "I had something I wanted to share with everyone before the group Mama left us for greener pastures." She pouted her lip at Violet. I reached over to wrap my arms around Violet, squeezing her. I had become closer to all the women here over the last few weeks, but Violet was the one who would go out of her way to sit next to me in company meetings. I don't know if it was because of her maternal instinct or because she was an empath. But when everyone else gave me space to grieve my breakup (mostly because I forced them to give me space), Violet didn't.

At first, I thought it was because she was new at work and didn't realize I had closed myself off for a while.

But no, Violet just didn't want me to feel alone. She's the one who reminded me of the nights Signe and the others would put together on occasion, reminding me of the time and place. She pushed me to enjoy existing as a single woman again.

Logically, I knew joining them would be good for me. When my parents passed, I saw a therapist a couple of times who really emphasized how important it was for me to find close friends. A social support group to help me through their loss.

Then I met Colleen, and she invited me into her social circle with wide-open arms. I didn't feel as lonely as I used to, but when we broke up, I suddenly didn't have that circle anymore.

I hated the feeling of feeling safe and supported, only to go back to loneliness immediately.

It was almost worse than just being lonely the entire time.

Part of my feelings was bitterness, I think. I was bitter at Colleen, her friends, and the world. I was bitter about everyone I had lost. I was bitter about being on my own.

But Violet didn't care. She saw how closed off I was and noticed how much distance I put between myself and my coworkers. After she gently encouraged me to hang out with our coworkers outside of work a few times, I realized something.

That these friends could be *mine*. And mine alone. I didn't need to date someone to have friends. I was capable of that. They wanted to be my friends.

It took me a while to wrap my head around it, but I wouldn't have been able to without Violet's friendliness at the office.

Because of that, I felt immensely grateful to her.

"I'm going to miss you all so much," Violet returned my hug, squeezing me tight. "I'm for sure going to intrude on your girls' nights via video calls, though."

"That would be great." Jacqueline smiled, sitting cross-legged as she pulled out an Oreo from the package Signe brought over.

"What did you want to announce?" Jamie asked Signe, bringing the conversation back.

Signe raised her dark red eyebrows at her, flicking her ponytail over her shoulder as she gave Jamie an amused look, "I don't know, did you want to announce your news first?"

Jamie's cheeks turned bright red.

Violet and I exchanged a look, wondering if we knew what the news was. Clearly, we both were in the dark. One glance at Jacqueline confirmed she was also lost; she lifted a shoulder in an "I don't know" gesture.

Mary was grinning like a Cheshire cat, though. After a moment of awkward silence, Mary reached over to grab Jamie's wrist. The one she kept tucked in her lap. When Mary lifted her girlfriend's hand for all of us to see, there was a collective gasp from the group when we all noticed what was on Jamie's ring finger.

A gorgeous golden ring with a dark red ruby.

"Oh my god!" Violet gasped, before leaning forward to inspect the ring. "You're engaged?"

"Yes," Mary sat a little taller, before kissing Jamie's hand and nuzzling her girlfriend's—sorry, *fiancée's*—hair, "I just asked her last night."

"And I said yes." Jamie was bright red from head to toe. She shyly tucked a strand of her pale blonde hair behind her ear while holding out her left hand for everyone to admire and *ooh* and *aah* over her engagement ring. Jamie was reserved, but even so, the joy on her face was palpable.

A sniffling sound was heard, and we all turned to face Signe. She had tears streaming down her cheeks that she desperately tried to wipe away with her hands, "I'm so happy for you two. This is the best day."

Mary's face softened before she released Jamie to wrap Signe up in a hug as well.

I *love* weddings. I always have. Some would argue that it wasn't very progressive of me, but I was a diehard feminist who also loved the idea of becoming legally bound to someone. Of having someone in your corner forever.

When I was a little girl, watching princess movies that

ended with women getting married and living happily ever after, I knew I wanted the same. But when I played with my Barbies, pretending women were the ones getting married to each other, eventually my mother caught on to the fact that I might be gay.

When I was about ten years old, telling her about a crush I had on a girl in my class, I remembered the look of heartbreak flickering over her face.

Not because her only daughter was a lesbian.

But because her only daughter wasn't legally allowed to marry whom she would fall in love with.

I could still vividly remember sitting in my apartment during college, receiving the news that gay marriage was legalized. I immediately locked my bedroom door to give myself time to fall into a sobbing mess on my bed. The little girl within me was cheering and clapping and making her Barbies kiss over and over again.

My sexuality wasn't illegal anymore.

I wasn't illegal anymore.

I could date women and tell them in the getting-to-know-you phase that I wanted to get married someday, instead of quietly knowing that it wouldn't happen.

It *could* happen now.

It was such a romantic concept to me.

It was a dream.

I immediately wanted to ask Mary and Jamie a hundred questions, but I refrained. They just announced their engagement to us. I doubted that they wanted to discuss dresses or catering or venues or dates quite yet.

"Okay, so that was our thing," Mary gestured between herself and Jamie as she released Signe and sat back in her seat. "What did you want to share, Signe?"

Signe sniffled, using the collar of her shirt to dab at her eyes as she giggled to herself.

"I feel silly saying this now," Signe murmured to herself before fanning her face with her hands, attempting to calm her emotions, "But...I'm pregnant."

Silence filled the room for half a second before everyone screamed with excitement.

Jacqueline covered her hands over her ears to shield herself from the unexpected noise, but her eyes and smile were wide with excitement.

"Oh my god!" I exclaimed, my gaze dropping to her soft belly. "Does Zaid know?"

Signe cackled, accepting hugs from Jacqueline and Jamie before turning to me, "Obviously, Zaid knows. I told him a couple of weeks ago."

"A couple of *weeks*?" Mary gasped, "And you're just now telling us?"

"We wanted some time to enjoy the news ourselves first," Signe lifted a shoulder, a warm smile touching her lips, "But we just told his family last night, so now I get to tell all of you."

"I have so many baby things I saved from Gracie if you need them," Violet offered. "It's probably a little early to offer that, but even when I'm up in northern California, I'll send you some stuff."

"You're so sweet. I'm going to be asking you all the questions about pregnancy and birth." Signe happily shook in her seat, "Oh my god, I'm so glad to *not* be keeping that secret anymore."

"But you're so *good* at keeping secrets," Mary teased. Signe rolled her eyes while all of us remembered the cringey and embarrassing circumstances that led to her and Zaid finally getting together. I wasn't working there at the time, but I heard the stories. The part about Jacqueline confronting Signe and Zaid about her book always made me want to turtle shell into my shirt from secondhand embarrassment.

Once all the hugs were given and all the snacks were distributed, everyone settled into the pile of blankets and pillows Signe often created for our movie nights. Aubrey Plaza's dry humor made everyone laugh, and I glanced around the room to take everyone in.

I was staring at Violet, whose blue hair was tied in a braid today, because I realized she and I were the only single women in the group. She caught me staring at her and raised her eyebrows in a silent question.

"I—never mind," I shook my head.

Violet scooted closer to me on the pillows, whispering, "Do you want to ask me about Taylor?"

My cheeks flamed.

Oh my god, did she know that Taylor and I—?

"They were texting you during our last session. I saw your name show up on their phone," Violet explained with an eyebrow wiggle.

"Ah, yeah, we texted." I nodded, still blushing. It suddenly felt very hot in here.

Violet grinned, "Do you think it's going to go anywhere?"

I shrugged.

The conversation paused while everyone else in the room laughed at another dry delivery from the characters in the movie. Once everyone had settled again, Violet turned to me.

"If it does turn into anything, let me know," Violet nudged me with her shoulder, "I want to keep up with all the gossip down here."

I grinned and nodded at her, "For sure."

It wasn't until everyone was focused back on the movie, and Mary was sound asleep on Jamie's lap, that I felt my phone buzz in my pocket.

Quietly tugging my phone out to check the notification, I felt a swarm of butterflies in my stomach from seeing the name lit up on my phone.

Taylor: I want to kiss you again.

Chapter Nine

TAYLOR

"HONEY, I'M HOME!" I called into the entryway of my parents' house.

As I slipped my sneakers off, I pulled my phone out of my pocket to see if Nicole had texted me back yet.

She hadn't.

It had been a whole day at this point.

Served me right, considering I also waited about a day to text her back that one time.

But this was different, because I was reaching out to her again after our very clear nothing-else-is-happening-here hookup. Even though she gave me permission to call her again. I mean, technically I texted her, but the intention was the same, wasn't it?

Maybe she felt put on the spot when I asked, and she just said yes to be nice?

When I left her apartment, I had every intention of waiting a few days before reaching out to her again. I had a feeling that Nicole was much shyer than I was and wouldn't reach out to me first. However, the next day, as I cleaned my apartment and went about my regular weekend routine, I realized that I was still waiting for her to text me.

Eagerly waiting.

Hopeful that she'd want to reach out to me, too.

I kept checking my phone, ignoring the notifications on a couple of dating apps I cycled through, ignoring the texts from my friends' group chat, trying to manifest that my phone was going to light up with Nicole texting me that she wanted me again.

I sat with those feelings for a bit, wondering if I was crossing some sort of boundary by wanting to hook up with her again. Or if I created some unrealistic, unfair fantasy where Nicole reached out to me first.

Her words from the day before kept playing in my mind: "I'm not sure what's next," and "I don't know the protocol."

Perhaps it was the *way* she said it.

Inexperienced with hookup culture, while knowing that I was very experienced in hookup culture.

I mean, Leo said it himself. I could be a great *rebound* for her. Everyone around me knew how I operated, so it made sense that Nicole would assume I wanted to get mine and move on in a reasonable amount of time.

What if...that wasn't all I wanted, though?

Obviously, I wanted to hook up with Nicole again. She was a beautiful woman, with a body that made me want to drool. Soft curves that felt amazing in my hands, a sweet smile that I wanted to kiss as much as I could, the tattoos on her arm that I wanted to study with uninterrupted intensity.

If Nicole was treating this like a strict hook-up with no strings attached, perhaps I needed to be the one to show her that I was okay with exploring the concept of strings.

Maybe, I don't know, one or two strings.

Just to start and see how things went from there.

So, I texted her.

And a day later, here I was, loitering in my parents' entryway, wondering if I was pushing her more than she wanted.

"In the kitchen!" My mom called, pulling me out of my thoughts.

I pocketed my phone with a heavy sigh.

I followed the smell of burgers and chips, and beer. My mom was ripping freshly washed lettuce into a big bowl. Her dark brown hair, streaked with grey, was pulled back into a bun. Her dark eyes hid behind her bright yellow glasses. She wore a romper today, making me suspect that she was gardening earlier. I could see my dad through the kitchen window, standing at the grill. When he and I made eye contact, he smiled and waved hello.

"Need help with anything?" I asked my mom.

She shook her head, nodding for me to take a seat on the countertop.

"I'm just finishing up the salad here," she replied, "How are you? It's been a few weeks since we've seen you."

I shrugged, "I'm good. Nothing new going on. Have you heard from Tucker lately?"

Tucker is my older brother by three years. He and his wife traveled more often than not.

"We video chatted yesterday. They had just settled into their Airbnb in Iceland."

"Ugh, I'm so jealous," I groaned, "I need to travel more."

"Us too," My mom smiled, "Your dad wants to see Thailand."

I tilted my head in question, "That feels out of left field."

"Not when you realize we've been watching season three of White Lotus."

"Ah," I nodded. That was usually where my dad got his

85

travel inspiration from. When *Game of Thrones* was airing, he wanted to travel wherever they filmed that season. Ireland, Spain, Iceland, Croatia, Malta, and even Morocco. When we asked why he wanted to go on a family vacation to Hawaii a few years ago, we learned that he had just watched *Mike and Dave Need Wedding Dates* and *Forgetting Sarah Marshall* and wanted to stay at the hotel where those movies were filmed.

My older brother Tucker and my dad shared the same travel bug.

My mom and I liked to travel, but we also liked lounging at home just as much.

"How was work today?" My mom asked.

"Good. I had one client take their first steps in my office today." I grinned as I stole a potato chip from a bowl on the counter. "I love experiencing those moments with the parents."

"How old is the client?" She asked.

"He's turning three next month," I replied. "His mom cried. She was worried he never would."

My mom stopped fixing the salad together to give me a wide-eyed look of appreciation, "That's so sweet. I'm glad all that kiddo's hard work is paying off."

"He met with Adam right after me for PT, too," I continued, "And showed off his new skills. It was the first time I've seen Adam get teary-eyed."

"What a big ol' softy," my mother chuckled. The sliding glass door to the backyard opened, revealing my dad holding a tray of freshly grilled meat.

"These might be my best turkey burgers yet." My dad puffed his chest out comedically as he presented the patties for my mom and me to awe over, his dark blue eyes that matched mine sparkled as he wiggled his dark eyebrows at the two of us, "You frickin' like that?"

Courtney taught him that.

It made me simultaneously laugh and die a little on the inside every time he said it.

"Yum," I grinned at the old man.

Just then, my phone buzzed on the countertop.

Both of my parents leaned over to glance at the name before I had time to snatch it off the table.

"Who's Nicole?" My dad asked.

I grinned at him before holding my phone close to my chest, relief from her response filling it.

I was insanely lucky.

My parents, as traditionally as they were raised, always had my back. When I was six years old and finally told my mom that I hated the dresses and skirts she would pick out for me to wear to school, she responded by cleaning them out of my closet and taking me clothes shopping for things that I preferred. Most of what I liked was in the boys' section. At first, they thought it was because I had an older brother and wanted to be like him.

To an extent, I did. I love my older brother.

My dad got excited to have an energetic, athletic child like me, since my older brother was more into the arts and had no interest in learning sports.

It wasn't until a couple of years later that I opened up to them again, letting them know that I didn't like it when they introduced me as their daughter. I was too young to have language for what I was experiencing, but my parents tried to adjust the best they could. For a couple of years, they referred to me as he/him or "their other son." I appreciated that because it gave me a chance to test it out for myself. To see if those words felt right for me.

It never quite felt right, though.

Over time, the words "he" and "him" started to feel off, a lot like "she" and "her" did. Like a square puzzle piece struggling to fit into a circle. It technically fit, but there was too much empty space left over. It felt like the square was too small for the space, a shape that only "worked" because it fell into the circle a little too easily. The puzzle of my identity felt incomplete.

I didn't want to feel incomplete.

Like I was settling for the square he/him puzzle piece out of convenience. I wanted to find the piece of the puzzle that was designed specifically for my kind of circle.

It was middle school when my parents sat me down to check in. They wanted to know if I needed anything else from them, or if there was anything they could do to help me feel more comfortable in my skin. They started talking to me about puberty blockers and being transgender. They had just met someone else at my school who identified as transgender and saw similarities between that child and me. But that didn't sit with me, either. I wasn't upset about starting my period, probably because I was never raised with the harmful, "Now you're becoming a woman," rhetoric around menstrual cycles. My parents taught me anatomy through a very scientific lens. They never correlated gender with what was between my legs.

My brother happened to have a penis, and he also happened to identify as a boy.

I happened to have a uterus and vagina, and my parents wanted to help me figure out my identity any way they could.

I remember wrinkling my nose at them in thought, before I finally said, "I don't think I'm a boy."

My mom tilted her head to the side in both acceptance and thought, "So what do you feel like you are?"

I took a moment to test the words in my head before I decided to say, "...I think I'm just Taylor."

My parents both looked at each other, smiled, and hugged me.

All of this was so new to them. To the people in our lives, and yet, they didn't see that as an excuse to brush me off—like so many other queer kids experienced.

My dad found an LGBTQ resource center an hour north of us in LA and he reached out to them for support. Through the center, we were able to find books and articles about being queer, the gender binary, and support groups for other kids and adults like me.

It was just before I started my freshman year at high school that I finally found peace in being non-binary.

"So instead of referring to you as 'he' or 'she', would you feel better if we referred to you as 'they'?" my dad asked. We were in his study, reading about non-binary individuals. The book I had in front of me had a lot of language that I wasn't familiar with yet, but I was completely absorbed. The LGBTQ center had to order it in. It discussed ancient cultures that thrived before colonization and didn't adhere to traditional gender binaries. I looked up from the book and responded to my dad.

"Could you test it out on me?"

My dad nodded, sat back in his seat, and pushed his reading glasses up his nose. "This is my youngest child, Taylor. They go to Orange Grove High School, and they like to play soccer and pull pranks on their older brother."

Something warm and safe settled in my chest.

All I had to do was nod my head, and the rest was history.

Near the end of high school, after discovering that I wasn't *just* attracted to women, but a variety of people I vibed with, I formally came out to my family as pansexual. When I did, my parents and brother just nodded at me.

"Makes sense," Tucker had told me, "You never cared what people looked like or what they identified as. But you've always cared about someone's character."

My dating history wasn't a thing my parents balked at. When I told them in my late twenties that I most likely wouldn't get married like Tucker, or have kids, they told me as long as I lived a happy life, that's all that mattered to them.

I could be open with them about who I was dating, how casual it was, etc. They never became those parents who were constantly asking their single kids, "When are you going to settle down?" or "Don't you feel lonely?"

They were already part of my support team.

I didn't need a monogamous romantic partner to not feel lonely.

My mom and dad understood that. They respected and trusted me to make my own judgments about romance, or the lack of romance. They were there if I had questions or just needed to vent. They never pushed me to get married or not. Perfectly supportive. Always loving.

Hell, I had it better off growing up enby and queer with my parents than Beck had it growing up straight with her religious parents. To my knowledge, Beck had only spoken to her parents once in the last decade because of the toxic expectations they continued to put on her in the name of their religion.

"Taylor?" My mom pressed.

I blinked back to the present, watching my parents gather food for us to sit and eat at the kitchen table.

"One sec," I lifted a finger as I followed them to the dining room, opening Nicole's text.

> Nicole: Are you free tonight?

Hell yeah!

> Me: Free as a bird. Want to come over?

"Is this someone new you're seeing?" My dad asked once we all got settled at the table.

"Yeah," I replied, resting my phone screen while I stabbed my salad with my fork, "We're making plans for tonight."

"Oh, what are you two going to do?"

In response, I silently chewed my food and stared at my mother with one raised eyebrow until it clicked.

"Oh, geez," she chuckled to herself, rolling her eyes as she continued, "That's what I get for asking."

I lifted a shoulder as my dad snorted and took a bite of his burger, which resulted in half of it being gone.

"Hey..." I took another bite of food and thought for a moment before I decided to be bold and ask, "...Did you two ever feel disappointed that I never got married or settled down?"

Both of them lifted their gazes from their plates to give me confused and alarmed expressions. The divot between my dad's dark eyebrows deepened dramatically, whereas my mom's eyes widened behind her frames.

"What? No, honey." My mom reached out and rested her hand on my arm. "Did we ever make you feel that way?"

"No, not at all." I lifted a shoulder, "I guess I was just curious. We've never really had a deep conversation about

91

it," I took a sip from the can of soda my parents set out for this meal, "I just told you one day that I wasn't interested in long-term relationships, and you both just, like, accepted that."

My dad hesitated before taking his next bite of salad, his fork hung halfway between the table and his mouth as he asked, "Did—did you want us to question you some more?"

My mom turned to look at me, waiting for my answer.

"No," I shook my head, "I love how you both trusted me to know what I want for myself. That you never pressured me one way or the other," I lifted my shoulder again, "But that doesn't mean you never had your own feelings about it."

They let my words hang over the table for a moment.

My parents shared another look, and part of me felt a little envious over how they could have silent conversations with each other so easily like this. My brother and I were pretty good at predicting what the other was going to say, but my parents had a connection that was deeper than I could fathom.

"I guess..." My mom set her fork down and folded her hands on the table in front of her, leaning closer to me, "Your father and I got extremely lucky. We found each other so young, and we grew up together. Not everyone gets to have that, whether they 'settle down' or not." My mom lifted her fingers in air quotes. "So when your father and I heard you say you weren't going to force anything like that to happen, and that you felt confident in that decision to live your best single life, we felt a little bit of relief."

I raised my eyebrows, "Why relief?"

"Taylor." My dad rested his elbows on the table as he folded his hands under his chin, "You've known what you wanted since the day you were born." He gave me a warm smile, the same one he'd been giving me for as long as I could remember. "You haven't made a lot of decisions that you've regretted in your life—big decisions, at least."

I smirked, remembering my stupid teenage years when my brother and I would get into typical teenage trouble.

"It's easy for young people to feel like they need to follow a step-by-step guide to thrive and be happy. Society does its hardest to convince people that they won't be happy unless they do A, B, and C. You, however, have always seemed immune to that."

I nodded at that because that's how I've felt, too.

"So that's why you felt relieved to hear me proclaim I was intentionally single?"

"We knew that nobody could pressure you to do anything you didn't want to do. So, when you said you weren't going to settle down and that you were happy, well, doing what you do," my mom continued, raising her eyebrows at me, "we felt relieved that you figured that out so young. If more people were as confident in themselves and their decisions as you are, I feel like the world would be a little less complicated."

I smiled at her, "That's nice of you to say."

"It's true." She sat straighter in her seat and started focusing on her food again.

"What if I ended up changing my mind?" I asked. *That* was what I had been thinking about ever since that kiss I shared with Nicole at the taco bar. This feeling of attachment. This feeling of wanting to be near her. Wondering what she was up to. The intoxicating thrill of learning that she liked me sexually, too.

I was expecting my parents to pause dramatically at my question.

Instead, they continued to eat as if this wasn't a big deal to them at all.

I was silly for expecting anything else.

"People are allowed to change their mind, Taylor," my dad spoke around his mouthful of turkey burger, "If you end up finding someone you want to settle down with, they must be special."

Shrugging, I thought about his words some more.

You hardly know Nicole, I reminded myself.

It was true, but—not to sound like Beck—I still felt something there. Something between us that I didn't think I had truly experienced until now.

Something scary, but exciting at the same time.

"Is Nicole someone special?" my mom asked, staring at my phone as it buzzed on the table.

I blushed, feeling like she was reading my mind.

"It's still very new, but..." I tilted my head back and forth, "...I think I really like her."

You hooked up one single time, calm the fuck down, T.

You know what, who the hell cares? Adam fell in love with Beck because he saw her laugh one single time before she even knew he existed. Nothing matters.

"Well, I hope you two have fun tonight." My mom hummed as she turned to my dad to ask about his day. While they started talking about his thrilling day of crunching numbers at the accounting firm he worked at, I finally read Nicole's text.

Nicole: Send me your address.

Chapter Ten

NICOLE

I JUMPED after Taylor opened their door.

It sounded like they ran to the front door after I knocked. I could hear the heavy thuds of their feet quickly approaching the door.

"Sorry, didn't mean to scare you," Taylor said, opening the door wide enough for me to step through the threshold into their apartment. I noticed a lot of muted warm colors. A burnt orange accent wall, healthy indoor plants on shelves. A large book with someone wearing a jersey on the cover, sitting on their wooden coffee table. Unlit candles on their kitchen counter to my right, a clean and empty kitchen sink. Cream curtains framing the sliding glass doors on the opposite end of the living space.

Their apartment was clean, cozy, and calm.

Being in their space made me want to relax my shoulders and dramatically exhale a sigh.

After they closed the door, they raised their hands to fix their hair.

Even though there was nothing wrong with it.

I wanted to run my fingers through it myself, though.

"Hi," I said as I slipped off my sneakers, "Cute jeans."

Taylor wore light-wash straight-leg jeans with a simple forest green t-shirt.

I liked how they looked in jeans. They looked good in their athletic wear, too. But something about jeans just did it for me. Their sock-covered feet tapped a rhythm on the floor as they shoved their hands in the pockets of their pants.

"Thanks, they're new," Taylor did a cute little twist, showing off their perfectly toned ass and how the jeans fit them like a glove.

"I'm a big fan." My eyes were glued on their ass until they twisted back and faced me straight on.

"This is good," Taylor smirked, before moistening their bottom lip with their tongue.

It reminded me of the last time they did that in front of me.

How they took my face and kissed me like their life depended on it.

We never made it to my bedroom that time.

Would we make it to their bedroom this time?

"Um," Taylor blinked and shook their head, looking a little lost in their own thoughts as well, "Can I get you anything? Water? Tea?"

I smiled, "Water would be nice, actually." I set my purse down next to my shoes, tucking my hair behind my ears in an attempt to cool off.

My heart was racing; my cheeks were flushed with both arousal and anticipation.

We both knew why I was here.

I wanted to hook up again.

They wanted to hook up again.

So, we were probably going to hook up again.

Would it be just as good as last time? Would the excitement wear off after this time?

"Here you go," Taylor's voice interrupted my spiraling thoughts as they slid a glass of filtered water over to me.

"Thanks," I smiled at them again before taking a few deep gulps of water. I ended up downing the whole glass, not realizing how thirsty I was, and appreciating how the refrigerated water cooled my body down a little bit.

Taylor took the empty glass from me; their calloused fingers gently teased my own before they refilled the glass again for me.

"Sorry," I huffed a laugh to myself, "I didn't realize how thirsty I was."

"No problem, hydrate or die-drate."

I snorted into my glass of water from their words. Water dribbled down my chin, and I choked on the water I was in the middle of swallowing.

Taylor's dark blue eyes sparkled, thrilled that they got me with that one.

I wiped my mouth with the back of my hand, swallowed the mouthful of water, and finished my sip. I shook my head at them, smiling widely.

"I haven't heard that one before."

"Glad I could be the first to share that age-old wisdom with you."

I laughed again, "Age-old? Is that what our ancestors said? Hydrate or die-drate?"

Taylor shrugged, before biting their lip and asking, "Nicole?"

"Yeah?"

"Can I have you now?"

My cheeks flamed at that question.

Something hot burned in my lower belly from their

words. My heart stopped in my chest and rapidly took off again. I wiped my hands on my own jeans, a looser fit than what Taylor wore, before I nodded.

"Are you sure?" Taylor asked. They turned their lips down in concern as they stepped closer to me, "Was that too forward of me? I'm sorry. You look nervous now. Do you want to do something else instead?" I had to hand it to them. They sounded genuine. As if I could say, "Actually, I want to watch all the extended versions of Lord of the Rings instead. That cool with you?" And they would probably respond with, "Sure, let me pop the popcorn." And it would be a normal turn of events.

But that wasn't what I wanted.

"You do make me nervous, but in an exciting way." I tucked my lips between my teeth, "I'm not used to such... directness."

Taylor's dark eyebrows twitched a little as they stepped closer. They held my eyes with theirs as they slowly looped their index fingers through my belt loops and tugged me closer to them.

"Let me know if I'm ever too blunt, okay?" Taylor's voice got quieter. Softer. Gentle.

"Okay." I nodded before resting my fingertips on their forearms. I slowly traced my fingers up toward their elbows, the outside of their biceps, before I slid a few inches up their shirt sleeves, "Also, yes."

"Yes?" Taylor asked, tugging me closer. Our jeans were flush together now. Their fingers looped on my beltloops, trapped between us.

"You—" I cleared my throat, "You can have me now."

Taylor smiled, wide and stunning.

Wordlessly, they released one of my beltloops but tugged me to follow them through their apartment with the other. Leading us toward their bedroom. I tried to take in as much of their bedroom as I could. Burnt orange comforter, wicker bedframe—unexpected, but it looked good. A clean wooden dresser with a lava lamp on it. No dust on their side tables. Sconces on either side of the bed.

Their calloused hand palmed my neck, dragging up toward my cheek to get me to look at them again. Their septum piercing glinted in the dim light of their room as they smirked at me.

I felt entranced by them. Like they could ask me to do whatever they wanted, and I would happily oblige. Something about them just...warmed me. I was nervous, a little awkward and stiff at first, but as soon as their lips pressed against mine again and they sighed, I felt my body respond similarly.

Kissing Taylor Desmond felt like finally filling your lungs with air. Like swallowing a mouthful of water after rationing. Kissing them felt like I was finally getting what I *needed*.

"I've needed this," Taylor murmured against me, as if they were inside my mind, "I missed you, Nicole."

I smiled against their lips, nipping their bottom lip with a confidence only they have been able to pull from me lately.

"I can't believe it's not just me," I whispered against their skin.

Taylor groaned before gently pushing me onto their mattress. The details of their bedroom were forgotten. All I could see was Taylor.

Their dark blue eyes were hooded and glassy and hypnotizing as they unbuttoned their jeans and pushed them down their strong and toned legs.

Taylor's dark hair flopped over their forehead, and they reached to undo mine and tug them off my softer legs.

"This okay?" Taylor asked, dragging their palms up my legs. Their eyes dropped to where I was aching for them.

"Yes. Please." I replied.

With a kiss on my thigh, they reminded me how easy it was for them to get me off. I wondered if the first time we got together was a fluke. A rarity. A result of being celibate for too long. But no, because they had just gotten off over a week ago, and I had gotten myself off every day since then— including this morning, but they were about to get me off within minutes *again*.

Their fingers were the perfect combination of gentle and teasing. When they lowered their lips to my center, I cried out.

"I'm almost there," I panted, my hands were balling up the comforter below me.

Taylor hummed their approval against me, and that's all it took.

While I throbbed around their fingers and moaned at the ceiling, I realized how crazy this was. How our chemistry was so undeniable. Our bodies responded to each other so easily, so simply.

This random human, whom I only met through a friend of a friend.

Perhaps it was meant to be, in a way.

I never believed in "the one," no matter how much of a romantic I was. But I did believe that there were certain types of people made for each of us. A small handful, sprinkled throughout the world, were designed for each other.

Even if Taylor and I were temporary, I appreciated whatever time we shared.

When they finally lifted their head from between my legs with a confident smile spreading on their cheeks, I fooled myself into believing that I could keep doing this.

That I could keep my heart out of the equation.

That we could be intimate and return to an amicable friendship, no problem.

I fooled myself, and I should have known better.

Chapter Eleven

NICOLE

WEEKS PASSED while a casual routine formed between Taylor Desmond and me.

We kept sleeping together.

It was still amazing every single time.

The best part was that Taylor had made it very clear how excited they were, too; it didn't feel completely one-sided.

At this point, Violet and her daughter had been living at Moore Farms for a while. Signe was helping Jacqueline interview candidates to take over her office manager position. Mary and Jamie started wedding planning. Everyone pretended that we couldn't hear Leo and Jacqueline making out in either of their offices during the workday.

I kept hooking up with Taylor.

Because *god*, it was so fun hooking up with Taylor.

But dangerous.

Because I *loved* spending time with them.

We would text each other daily. I was shocked at how quickly our relationship went from casually fucking to sending each other memes and news articles, but it happened.

I looked forward to seeing them, not just because of all the orgasms they could ring from me with no more than a look and a steady hand.

It wasn't until we were hooking up at my place and focusing on how much I loved being the one to drive them over the edge, that I realized I might need to reevaluate how involved I was with them.

I had Taylor practically pinned to my bed, both of us completely naked, while I worked them over with my mouth. They had their hands gripping the edge of my headboard while they bit their bottom lip and their cheeks flushed.

"I'm so close, babe," Taylor murmured as they squeezed their eyes closed.

This whole time, we continued to call each other pet names.

But this time, something went off in the back of my mind.

It sounded too real, too familiar now, after weeks of this pattern.

As if they belonged to me, and I belonged to them.

Eating Taylor out was mind-altering because, for a few moments, I was performing as if we were each other's to claim. As if I were the only one that they ever wanted to receive this attention from. Completely submissive under me, whimpering from my ministrations. Their naked chest and neck were flushed because only *I* was the one who could see them like this.

Even though we talked about other things, interests, tastes in food, and mutual pet peeves, we never talked about what either of us wanted out of this. Or didn't want out of this?

"Fuck," Taylor groaned as I teased their clit with fast and steady flicks of my tongue. They didn't like to feel stretched, only stimulated. The pads of my two fingers were curling inside of them, teasing that rough patch of nerves that I knew would send them over the edge soon.

While I watched them writhe underneath me, I was surprised I hadn't collapsed yet. They had already given me three earth-shattering orgasms before this.

C'mon, Taylor, I chanted in my head, *give me this, at least.*

When they fell apart underneath me, I memorized every aspect of them I could. Every gasp. Every whimper. Every rise and fall of their flat chest. Every flex of their toned stomach. The taste of their tart arousal on my tongue.

I worked them as much as they worked me.

After orgasm number three, they shook their head at me and gently pushed me away from them.

I lifted my head to smile at them, licking my lips.

Taylor whimpered, reached forward. They pulled me up against their chest. They tucked my head under their chin, pulled the covers over us, and wrapped their arms around me. My leg fell between theirs, and we rested in each other's embrace for a few moments.

"Just let me breathe with you for a little bit," Taylor whispered against my hair.

We'd cuddled after sex plenty of times before.

Taylor was very adamant about aftercare, which I appreciated.

We'd fallen asleep together a handful of times now, but usually they would wake up and kiss my forehead goodbye. They liked to get up early and go on a run before their workday, and they didn't want their morning schedule to disrupt mine.

Part of me wondered if that's what kept this relationship between us so casual.

So, the next morning made me question our relationship even more.

Because we woke up in bed, still completely wrapped up in each other.

It felt way more intimate than anything we did together the previous night.

Even more terrifying, it felt *right*.

WE BRUSHED our teeth in my bathroom together.

Taylor didn't go on a run. They stuck around.

Both of us were awkward and somehow...not awkward at all. We kept glancing at each other in the mirror, smirking and blushing over nothing.

Should I bring up what I was thinking?

How the pattern of us sleeping together like this for a couple of weeks was starting to plant ideas in my head? Ideas that may or may not have merit, depending on where they stood?

I had no problem asking if Taylor wanted to borrow a spare toothbrush I had stored under my sink, but the thought of asking them, "What are we?" seemed too nerve-wracking to handle.

I needed to talk to them.

About what we were doing, where each of us saw this going.

How I was a relationship person, and doing the casual

thing for too long might not be a good idea for the romantic in me.

Plus, we had a lot of mutual friends. Perhaps it was best not to leave the discussion open at all and instead bring up the fact that we should take a break from each other. Stopping whatever was forming between us now, amicably, seemed like a better alternative to getting too attached, only for them to move on to someone else, and accidentally break my heart.

I wanted to keep going to Leo's rugby games with Jacqueline, without being haunted by memories Taylor and I had together.

So, yes, it made the most sense for me to end things now before I started entertaining the idea of Taylor and I being an item.

As soon as that thought crossed my mind, a sour rock formed in my gut.

I hated that idea.

Which put me right back at square one.

"Nicole?" Taylor asked me after rinsing their mouth out in the sink.

I was in the middle of applying the moisturizer that Taylor said they used every morning. I was determined to look as youthful as them at thirty-nine.

"Yeah?" I asked, massaging the cream into my cheeks.

"Can we go on a real date?"

I froze, giving them a curious look in the mirror.

What the hell?

I was completely caught off guard.

"A real date?" I asked, making sure I heard them correctly.

Taylor was styling their hair with some mousse and their fingers, looking casual as they elaborated.

"Yeah." They lifted a shoulder, and I almost felt gaslit over how casual they were acting. As if the "they have flings" person wasn't formally asking me out on a date. "...I want to take you out. I think we're good together." After that, they rinsed their fingers off in the sink, giving me a nervous look, "...Do you?"

I took a moment to study their face, because yeah, they looked *nervous* now.

So, I wasn't completely crazy for being surprised by this request.

I blushed, but I couldn't stop the smile that curved the corners of my mouth.

"I—yeah. We're good together," I nodded, rinsing my toothbrush out in the sink, "...I like you."

Taylor grinned at me in the bathroom mirror, "I like you too, gorgeous."

I tucked my lips between my teeth, low-key appreciating this unexpected turn of events.

But there was still a big, fat elephant in the room, I just couldn't ignore anymore.

They have flings.

"Taylor?" I asked.

"Yeah, babe?"

My heart expanded in my chest; it was almost hard to breathe, but I was a grown woman. I forced myself to move past the thrill of hearing them call me that and focus on my question.

Except I didn't ask a question.

There was a disconnect between my brain and mouth.

Because what I said instead was, "I want to get married someday."

Oh my god, that *is what I decided to say.*

Taylor paused, raising an eyebrow at me in the mirror, "...Okay..."

Fuck. I just ruined this.

"...Can we go on a date first?"

I closed the toilet lid and sat down, resting my elbows on my legs, hiding my burning cheeks in my hands, "I don't know why I said that. I'm so sorry. That's not—I mean. It's not wrong. But I'm not proposing to you right now."

"Don't apologize." Taylor shook their head at me before crouching in front of me and clasping my wrists in their hands. They slowly removed my hands from my face and looked at me.

"It's just—Colleen would argue that it isn't super feminist of me. I mean, marriage isn't the most logical route nowadays unless you're looking for some underwhelming tax benefits," I tried to explain, "But I'm a romantic. This is the first time I've jumped into a sexual relationship without defining the expectations first. I've loved the idea of growing old with someone since it, you know, became a possibility..."

Taylor nodded, letting me ramble at them as I struggled to gather my thoughts.

I inhaled a deep breath, forcing myself to be brave and say what I was thinking.

"...But I know that's not really how you function..."

It was quiet for a moment.

Then, Taylor pulled at my wrists, tugging me off the toilet and into their lap. My legs naturally wrapped around them as they leaned back on their heels. My butt rested on their thighs as they wrapped their arms around my waist.

"That's not how I've done things in the past," Taylor murmured against my hair, "But...I'm allowed to change my mind."

I froze in their hug, trying to remember to breathe, "Oh."

"Also," Taylor leaned back at me and gave me a disbelieving look, "You can love the idea of marriage and still be a feminist. Do you think everyone should get married? That they won't be happy until they do?"

I frowned at them, "No. That's just what I want for me."

Taylor nodded, "Then you're still a feminist. You believe women should make that choice for themselves. But can I tell you something?" They released their hold on my waist to cup both of my cheeks in their palms. Their thumbs brushed against my cheeks, "I still want to go on a date with you. Get to know you better."

I sighed, "But—that's my point—if you're not interested in anything long term—"

"I am." Taylor interrupted me.

I slammed my lips closed.

My heart stopped.

Did I hear them right?

"You—you are?"

Taylor sighed, adjusting their hold on me.

"You're right. I haven't been interested in anything long term...before *you*," Taylor explained while a light pink stained their cheeks, "But with you...I don't know. Maybe I should spiral about this more. Maybe I'm rushing into things as someone who has operated as aromantic for most of their life. But this is also how I've *always* operated. I realize I want something, and if it feels right in my gut, I go for it."

I widened my eyes at that.

Clearing my throat, I asked, "And what do you want...?"

"I like you, Nicole," Taylor replied with a smirk, "Like, *really* like you. So much so that I'm selfishly glad your ex cheated on you because then I had a chance to show you how you should be treated. I want to show you what you deserve. I want to *date* you. When I'm not with you, I am counting down the days until I can be with you again. So," They pecked my lips once, quickly. "Knowing where I stand, what my intentions are...can I take you out tonight?"

I could hear my heartbeat in my ears.

Feel it in my neck and in my wrists.

I nodded but also decided I should clarify with words.

"Yeah. Let's go out tonight—if this is what you want."

Something softened in Taylor's eyes as they stared at me.

"I want you," Taylor replied, "More than I have wanted someone ever."

I bit my bottom lip, and they raised one of their hands to tug it free with their thumb.

I smiled at the touch.

"Okay."

They gave me a wide smile in return, "Okay."

Chapter Twelve

NICOLE

ANOTHER TRAIT that made me basic in my ex's eyes?

I love flowers.

Roses. Lilies. Daffodils. Daisies.

God, *especially* daisies.

Our date wasn't extravagant; it was simple. Taylor drove us down to Laguna Beach, a few blocks away from where they had rugby practice. We got pizza at a small hole-in-the-wall shop I wouldn't have noticed had I been exploring on my own and then we got dessert at a gelato shop around the corner. After, because we were both so full, we decided to play tourist and explore all the small shops that were scattered along the Pacific Coast Highway.

It was so laid back and low pressure.

It was perfect.

I was on a bit of a high when we walked by a florist, and I was suddenly hit with the perfume of flowers.

There was a bouquet of yellow daisies. Right there in the front of the shop. Waiting for me.

I tapped Taylor's arm to let them know I was stopping.

"What is it?" They asked. Their hands were shoved in

the pockets of their faded jeans. As they saw me approach the bouquet outside the little shop, I tried not to feel too embarrassed.

"These are so pretty," I practically sighed as I traced the perfectly bloomed flower petals. Taylor was quiet as they stood at my side, letting me admire them, "You're coming with me." I informed the flowers.

Taylor laughed, "You're getting them?"

My hackles rose. I tried to relax my shoulders, "I am. I love these."

My words were firm. Unapologetic. Confident.

"Hell yeah," Taylor replied.

I grinned before plucking the bouquet from the bucket they resided in and striding through the shop.

Someone else was completing their purchase in front of me, so I waited behind them. The store had a lot of trinkets, lots of touristy magnets and buttons, and things. There were shells, macabre items, candles, and vases filled with sand.

Shops like these are always scattered across the streets in beach towns like this.

When I felt Taylor's presence beside me, I turned to look up at them, momentarily surprised to see what was in their hands.

"Let me," Taylor reached into their back pocket with their free hand, pulling out their wallet.

"What do you mean?" I asked, staring at the matching bouquet of daisies they held.

"I want to buy these for you," Taylor fidgeted with their wallet, a brief look of nerves coated their features as they dragged their dark blue eyes over to me, "Is that alright? Can—can I buy you flowers, Nicole?"

My heart was fluttering in my chest.

Heat rose to my cheeks.

I couldn't remember the last time someone bought me flowers.

I had no issue buying myself flowers. I didn't do it as often as I would have liked, but I was familiar with picking out my own.

Taylor, however, was standing tall next to me, holding a matching bouquet. Doubling the number of flowers I could bring home.

"Yeah," I nodded, "You can buy me flowers."

"You sure?" Taylor looked pleased, if the way their lips quirked up on the sides meant anything.

Their words from our intimate conversation on my bathroom floor that morning rang in my head.

They wanted *me*.

"Yes," I nodded, snuggling my bouquet to my chest.

Taylor nodded once and stepped forward.

The person ahead finished, and it was our turn.

"Just these?" the woman behind the counter asked.

"Yes, please." I nodded. Taylor looped one of their fingers through the belt loop of my shorts, tugging me closer before they flipped open their wallet to pay.

"Unless you have more yellow daisies in the back?" Taylor inquired.

I snickered, "No, no. These are plenty." I leaned into them. My chest felt both heavy and light at the same time.

"You sure?" Taylor asked, before bending down and briefly kissing the crown of my head.

"Positive." I was grinning as they handed their card over to the cashier.

"You can never have too many." The cashier shrugged, "Your partner seems fun."

"They are." I smiled up at Taylor, who smiled down at me in return.

After that, they took my hand, and we continued walking through the beach town. We had just come to a large hill, and while I was focusing on what it was going to be like walking back up the damn thing, Taylor tugged me in a different direction, near some buildings on the left side of us.

"Come with me," Taylor muttered, leading me through small shops and alleys.

I laughed; low-key loving being dragged on a side-quest with them.

Another turn, and we were standing behind a block of tourist shops. Bare brick walls with little to no artwork were now behind us, but in front of us was a breathtaking sight.

"...Wow..." I breathed.

It was sunset, the sky was painted in oranges and pinks and warm colors that sparkled over the Pacific Ocean. There wasn't a beach in front of us, just the cliffside with lots of foliage scattered down it until it became rocks.

We were behind the tourist shops that were scattered along the very edge of the cliff, giving us an unobstructed view of the sunset.

A handful of clouds blocked the sun itself, making it so that I didn't need to squint to enjoy the view.

"Not bad, huh?" Taylor smirked, tugging me to sit on the ground. We sat with our backs against the brick wall of a bakery, sweets perfumed the air, mixing with the salt of the ocean in front of us.

"What a view," I smiled at them with my words, loving how they leaned their body against mine as much as possible. We leaned into each other's warmth against the cool ocean breeze.

I pulled out one of the daisies from the bouquets we just

bought and started fidgeting with it in my fingers as I broke the silence we had settled into.

"So..." I focused on the daisy in my hand while a nervous smile tugged at my lips, "This is what it's like to go on a date with Taylor Desmond."

Taylor laughed, rubbing a hand over their face once before they turned to give me a hooded look with their eyes, "This is what it's like to go on a date with Nicole Young."

I snickered.

"...I pegged you for a chill date kind of gal," Taylor added.

I raised my eyebrows at that, "You're not wrong, but what gave you that idea?"

Taylor smirked at me before responding, "Remember Jacqueline's dance at rugby?"

I nodded. It was a grand gesture of sorts, from my understanding. I was mostly excited to call the group of women at work my friends. I was just happy to be invited to watch the whole thing.

"You were secondhand embarrassed the entire time," Taylor snickered.

I widened my eyes at them, "How could you tell?"

They gave me a disbelieving look before shaking their head, "You have no poker face, babe. It was obvious you appreciated how sweet it was, but as I watched you watch Jacqueline shake her ass for Leo in front of our team, you looked like you wanted to crawl into a hole."

I barked out a laugh because they were completely right.

"So, that translates to me liking laid-back dates?" I asked.

"I translated that to mean, though you like gestures, you don't like big showy ones. It would make sense that you felt the same about first dates. Nothing crazy, nothing exotic. Just... connection. Intimacy." Taylor lifted a shoulder.

I stared at them, shocked that they thought about a singular moment for so long, so accurately, that they could get a read on me from it.

"What kind of dates do you like, then?" I asked, snuggling against them. I rested my head on their shoulder, and they plucked the daisy from my hand to tuck it behind my ear.

"I like being active." Taylor smiled against me, pressing their forehead against mine, "Going on hikes, playing pickleball, strolling Laguna Beach with a handful of flowers." I lifted my head to look at them more directly.

"Do you want to keep moving? There's a ton of new shops here, we could—"

Taylor stopped me with a kiss, a quick peck, just enough to get me to stop talking.

"I like this," they whispered, resting their forehead against mine. They slipped one of their legs under both of mine, somehow bringing us even closer. "I like walking around, and I like having this quiet moment, too." They plucked a daisy from one of the bouquets, tucking it behind their own ear. We now had matching daisies, "I like hearing your soft laugh. I like watching your smile pull against your cheeks, revealing your cute little smile lines." I tried to fight it, but I blushed and smiled widely at that, tilting my head down against theirs, "I like getting you to open up to me more, even though your last relationship didn't end well."

I bit my lip, looking up at them under my lashes. They were a little blurry this close to my face, but I felt safe with them. Hidden behind a building, the noise of the waves protected our conversation from anyone who might discover us back here.

"I'm...scared of this. Us." I admitted.

Taylor licked their lips in thought.

"Because of your ex?"

I lifted a shoulder, "Because we have mutual friends."

They leaned back a little bit, not out of shock, but curiosity. They waited silently for me to elaborate.

So, I did.

"You and I get along so, so well." I whispered, "Our chemistry is obviously there." I released a small laugh, but Taylor only smiled, waiting for me to continue. Not bouncing on the opportunity to change the subject to something sexual and flirty. "You're so different from me, and yet, I..." I inhaled a breath for bravery, "I feel like we just...fit."

Taylor exhaled at that, blinking once before asking, "And our mutual friends?"

I pressed my lips together to keep them from trembling too much before I continued, "I lost all my friends when Colleen cheated on me..." I inhaled a shaky breath before I elaborated, "They were all her friends first, before she started dating me. So, even though she was the one who cheated, when it came down to choosing sides...I wasn't chosen."

"Oh, babe." Taylor wrapped me in their arms, pressing a firm kiss to the crown of my head, making sure not to mess with the daisy in my air, "I'm so sorry."

I sniffed, accepting their comfort as I wrapped my arms around them too and spoke against their shoulder, "I finally feel like I'm forming my group. Friends. Maybe even family, but...if you and I...if we don't..."

"I totally get it," Taylor murmured against my head, "I understand your hesitation."

I leaned back, trying to compose myself. "You do?"

"Yeah," Taylor gave me a comforting smile, "I'm not going to try to convince you that it won't ever happen, because I don't know the future. But...believe me when I tell you that I *don't* want that to happen. I also don't think our friends are so emotionally immature that they'd feel the need to 'pick sides' between us."

I nodded, pecking their lips once.

I loved that they were having this conversation with me on the first date.

I loved that I felt safe enough expressing my perspective toward them, without the fear of them weaponizing it against me later.

"Thank you for listening." I nodded, "I like you. A lot. And...it's scary liking someone a lot after, well..."

"Being treated the way you were," Taylor finished for me.

"Yeah," I agreed.

We sat there in comfortable silence, my concerns floating around us, not like a looming threat, but as a simple reality. Something to be acknowledged and respected but not intimidated by.

"Well," Taylor sighed, settling us back against the brick to admire the darker sky, "I guess the only thing to do from here is keep dating the shit out of each other."

I snorted, "That's it? Just like that?"

God, how were they so relaxed and carefree all the time?

Taylor smiled, their profile lit up from the setting sun, reflecting off their septum ring, "Just like that."

The more I got to know Taylor Desmond. The more time I spent with them and the more conversations we shared, the more I felt like I had finally *found* something. Something I *thought* I knew how to find in the past. Something that escaped me in a way I had no concept of understanding, until I could finally see it in its reality. Feel it. Comprehend the truth of it. It was an overwhelming feeling of finally standing in front of something I had been seeking my entire adult life. Now that I could visualize it in front of me, understanding the reality of what I was missing somehow seemed bigger.

Scarier.

Every aspect, every detail I learned about Taylor, made me feel like they were stitched together in complete perfection. So different than me, and yet so *right* for me.

It was as if the universe was finally, finally throwing me a bone.

Here is this person, she was telling me, in all her glory, *you will fall in love with every part of them. Every perfection, every flaw. You thought you understood love before? You have no idea what you're in for. They are tailored specifically to you. For you.*

I just hoped, with everything I had left in me, that I could be tailored for them.

Chapter Thirteen

TAYLOR

On my phone screen, Violet reached behind herself to tie her hair up before settling into her spot on the stool, "Okay, I'm ready."

I nodded, glancing up briefly when Nicole tiptoed out of my bedroom toward the kitchen. She wore nothing but a shirt and cheeky panties, and god, she was gorgeous.

We'd gone on an official date once a week on average since our first date over a month ago. We went on more walks, on a hike, to the movies, even to a paint-and-sip art class that we both agreed never to do again.

But our poorly painted trees were now proudly hanging in Nicole's apartment.

We were more comfortable staying the night at each other's houses.

Each night, whether we were saying goodbye and going to our own apartment or snuggling in bed together for a sleepover, we would check in with each other.

"I like you."

"I like you, too."

It was a brief conversation.

Easy.

Until it wasn't, because last night, I realized I wanted to change it up just a smidge.

Because falling in love with Nicole Young was one of the easiest things I had ever done.

How to tell her, though?

Would she trust me when I finally said those words to her?

I didn't want to rush her. Her trauma and how her last relationship ended would probably play a role for a while. It's difficult for people to heal from being cheated on. The trauma could last years.

Knowing that, I still wanted to be there for her through it all.

I focused back on Violet, her picture filling the screen on my cellphone. I had forgotten that she and I scheduled this call this morning. When my phone started buzzing, I tried to slip out of Nicole's arms without waking her.

That obviously didn't work, because Nicole was tiptoeing around my call.

I cleared my throat and spoke to Violet, "The first question they'll probably ask you is, what kind of behaviors does Gracie struggle with at home and in school?"

Violet gnawed on her lip, and even though Violet was attractive in her own way, I realized how that movement didn't do anything to my insides, unlike when Nicole bit her bottom lip. I usually ended up wanting to bite it myself.

"Since we've moved, her mouthing has increased a lot." Violet's gaze drifted to the side as if seeing the behaviors she remembered. "She is quicker to bite her arm or her shirt when she's stressed."

Violet was starting the process of trying to see if Gracie qualified for one-on-one support in her kindergarten class. She asked me for pro tips on what to expect when the district psychologist called to ask her about Gracie's behaviors, because I had learned a lot about this through my line of work.

I nodded, watching Nicole return from the kitchen with a glass of water in her hand. "Does Gracie elope?"

Violet shrugged, "Yeah, eloping has increased too. But she's also improved in so many other ways—" I lifted a hand to cut her off.

"That's not what I asked you."

Nicole raised an eyebrow at me as she took a sip from the glass, leaning against the wall and crossing one of her slender ankles over the other. Her toes were painted bright yellow.

"What?" Violet's voice made me focus back on my video call.

"Don't offer them more information than what they ask for." I forced my eyes away from the beauty standing in my apartment and back on my blue-haired friend, "All I asked was if Gracie eloped. All you need to respond with is 'Yes.'"

Violet nodded, "Yes. Gracie elopes."

"At home? At the store?" I pressed.

"Both. And also—wait—" Violet's brows pinched, "Do I go into detail here? Or will that also kill the deal, so to speak?"

"It doesn't hurt to expand when you're making it sound like Gracie's eloping is a real problem you deal with often."

Violet nodded, "I feel a little bit like I'm lying. I mean, Gracie *does* have all these behaviors, but focusing on those feels unfair to all the progress she's made in other areas."

"I know." I shifted back, propping my feet up on the

coffee table and holding my arm out toward Nicole. She raised both of her dark eyebrows at me this time, tentatively stepping toward me.

I made direct, unblinking eye contact with her until she fulfilled my silent request.

Sit with me. Be with me. You're safe.

Nicole smiled and gently sat her cute little ass on the farthest cushion from me, keeping herself out of the frame of Violet's call.

"What you need to realize, my sweet wholesome Violet—"

I was interrupted by a humorous snort from her end, "If only you knew how *not* sweet and wholesome my mind has been lately."

I widened my eyes, "I'm coming back to that. But my point is, that you're not lying to the district about Gracie's struggles. You have good reason to want to increase her one-on-one support hours during the school day. The issue you're dealing with is that school districts like this will always, *always* want to cut corners when it comes to their special ed programs. So, if you list all of Gracie's behaviors, but then try to put a band-aid over them by saying, 'But she's improved with her AAC in the last month,' then the district will take that as an opportunity to hit you back with, 'Well, see? Her communication skills are still improving, so we don't need to pay for her to have more support.'"

Violet frowned before scraping her fingernails through her scalp, "Fucking fuck."

Nicole started making hand gestures from her spot on the couch, and I tilted my head at her in confusion, "What?"

"I didn't say anything else," Violet replied from my phone.

Nicole blushed and started waving her hands around again and mouthing words I couldn't interpret.

"What are you saying?" I asked, still confused.

"Who are you talking to?" Violet asked.

"Nicole," I replied.

Nicole slammed her mouth shut; a beautiful blush stained her cheeks as she widened her eyes at me in shock.

"Oh—hi Nicole!" Violet waved and leaned closer to her phone.

Nicole covered her face with her hands and slouched on the couch. I realized Nicole wasn't wearing pants yet and refrained from panning my phone over to her.

"Wait, wait," Violet narrowed her eyes at me, "Why is my CFO at your place at eight-thirty in the morning—" Violet's jaw dropped suddenly before she transformed her face into a mischievous grin and started wiggling her eyebrows, "You two had a sleepover, didn't you?"

"Yup," I smirked when Nicole grabbed a throw blanket off the back of the couch and covered herself up completely in it, squirming, "Nicole is being timid about it, though."

"Why?" Violet rolled her eyes before cupping her hands around her mouth and saying, "You're allowed to have sleepovers, Nicole!"

"I know *that*." Nicole's voice was muffled under the blankets before she poked her head out, and because she was now sufficiently covered, I turned the phone toward her so she could speak to Violet directly. "I just didn't realize we were telling our mutual friends about our sleepovers. That's all."

You have nothing to worry about, I wanted to tell her, *I love you too fucking much to lose you, mutual friends or not.*

"I can't believe my CFO and Gracie's OT are doin' it,"

Violet giggled, "I'm *so* sex deprived. Please tell me everything. Have you been seeing each other for a while?"

"Why are you sex deprived?" Nicole asked, sitting up a bit more. She finally scooted closer to me so I could wrap an arm around her slender shoulders, pulling her snugly against my body.

She fit so perfectly there.

When she adjusted the throw to cover some of my legs as well, I even sighed with contentment.

"Ugh," Violet groaned and threw herself back in her chair, clearly forgetting she was sitting at a kitchen island and not a bed or couch. She almost fell backward, giggling at herself when she stabilized and focused back on the conversation, "This stays between the three of us, especially you, Nicole."

Nicole snuggled closer to me, "Okay."

On the screen, Violet made a show of checking her surroundings to make sure the room was empty before she leaned close to her phone. So close, we could only see her eyes and forehead, "I'm so, *so* horny for Brandon's brother."

"What!?" Nicole laughed, shaking the two of us, "What's his name again? Grayson or something?"

"His name is Graham," Violet whispered into the phone, "And I've never wanted a man to be inside of me more."

I snorted at the same time Nicole laughed with a grimace, wrinkling her nose in disgust, "Violet. He's our client. And Brandon's brother. You can't."

Violet squeezed her eyes closed, still comically close to her phone camera, and pretended to sob, "I know, I know. But it's been so long since I've *wanted* sex—parenting, you know? Plus, my dad lives with us, and no way in hell am I bringing a guy home with my dad sharing a wall—but everything he does is *so* attractive. For literally no reason.

I'm *constantly* popping bean. The number of times I've had to charge my vibrators this last month is chilling."

Nicole was still giggling against me, "They'll have to do for now. I can't recall the specifics of our contract with Moore Farms, but I'm pretty sure 'don't sleep with the CEO's brother' is implied."

Violet thumped her head down on her kitchen island, giving us a nice view of her electric blue hair falling all over the marble.

"You don't have to worry. I'm under the impression that the horny-ness isn't exactly reciprocated." Violet murmured against the island.

"His loss," I shrugged. "He's missing out on your massive mommy-milkers."

"Damn straight," Violet sat up and pulled the collar of her V-neck shirt down, pushing her breasts together as she smiled down at her own cleavage, "The universe blessed me with glorious tits after having Gracie, and only men who are completely obsessed with me get to motor-boat them."

Nicole was laughing against my side, covering her mouth with her hand. I squeezed her closer and didn't hold myself back from dropping my nose to her hair and inhaling. God, she smelled so good. The memories from last night were still fresh in my mind, and I wondered if she was enough of a morning person to be up for another round.

"Do you have any more questions for me, Violet, or—"

"*Ohmygod* you have to see this!" Violet was whispering again, her gaze locked on something off-screen. The image of her pixelated for a moment while she moved, thumping over to a new area in her kitchen, "Are you fucking kidding me with this shit?"

"What?" Nicole and I both asked in a whisper.

Violet flipped the camera, and soon, we were looking

through a window. You could tell she was adjusting the camera to avoid the blinds being in the way, but she didn't want to open them that much and be spotted.

"Whoa, is that him?" I asked, leaning forward a bit.

A few yards away from Violet's (thankfully clean) kitchen window was the bare back of a man with blonde hair. It fell to his shoulders, and the top half of his hair was pulled back into a man-bun. An axe appeared over his shoulder before he swung it down on a stump, splitting the large log in one hit.

There was a small pile of stacked wood to one side, and a small pile of logs that hadn't been split yet on his opposite side.

"This is cruel," Violet whispered, "He does this a few times a week. More often on weekends." She sighed, and Nicole snorted.

"Is that his house?" Nicole asked, leaning forward. Violet's phone panned over to a black log cabin-style home. There wasn't a fence separating Violet's house and the black-painted one, but they were too far apart to be in the same building.

"We're next-door neighbors, much to his chagrin." Violet snickered. "Our primary bedrooms both have outdoor decks that face each other. He can't escape me." She ended her sentence with a low, comically evil laugh.

"That cabin looks so magical," Nicole's voice sounded dreamy, so I immediately filed away that bit of information about her, right next to all the other cute little facts I've learned about her.

Nicole experiences with secondhand embarrassment.
Nicole loves guacamole.
Nicole scrunches her nose when she's grossed out.
Nicole's parents both passed away.

Nicole is an only child.

Nicole is scared to lose her new friends at work.

Nicole gets nervous whenever I bring up introducing her to my friends.

Nicole prefers to be the little spoon.

Nicole gravitates toward the color yellow, like me.

Nicole thinks modern-looking cabins are dreamy.

In my brain, I collected these pieces of information into a bedazzled jar labeled "Nicole" and slid them underneath my bed until I needed them.

"Come visit!" Violet whispered. The camera blurred, and her wide green eyes filled the screen again, "I need a bestie's day."

"I'll check my schedule," Nicole trailed her fingertips along my thigh, out of sight from my phone's camera. Goosebumps erupted on my exposed skin, and I suddenly had the urge to rip my athletic shorts off and ask Nicole to tease me with her fingertips everywhere.

I craved her physical touch more than anything.

Violet asked me a few more questions regarding her phone call with Gracie's school district before we said goodbye.

Instead of inquiring about breakfast, Nicole snuggled into me some more. She adjusted her position so her back was mostly against my side, so she could mindlessly scroll on her phone with both hands.

I stared at her.

Casually lying on me like this.

It was a form of cuddling we'd engaged in more and more over the last few weeks.

Casual. Intimate. Safe.

Suddenly, the sound of Joshua Madey singing filled the quiet space. I thought it came from my phone, since sometimes he'll break into song on a call. I was just starting to wonder how my phone answered his call without me noticing it, when I realized the song wasn't coming from my phone at all.

It was coming from Nicole's.

My body stiffened under hers.

Oh.

One look at her phone, gave me a clear visual of a video clip of Carbon Cut performing years ago.

It was a clip of Josh swallowing a bug at an outdoor event mid-song.

I'd seen it numerous times, because, after it happened, I shoved it in Josh's face every time I could. I constantly teased him about it. I would walk into the townhome without a word, just my phone out, showing him messing up his biggest hit mid-song by swallowing a bug and hacking up a lung in front of thousands.

I would randomly cast it on their TV mid-conversation.

I played it in front of him so often after it happened that baby Susie had learned how to fake cough to get a laugh out of the adults around her.

What was the point of being best friends with the most famous rock star in the world if I couldn't give him shit when he messed up on stage?

Nicole glanced up at me with her dark eyes, smiling widely, before seeing my face. Something she saw made her smile dim.

"Sorry, sorry," she turned the volume down on her phone, but let the video replay again. Her body shook with a restrained giggle at Josh turning away from the audience and loudly smacking his chest. Garrett, the lead guitarist, pointed and laughed at Josh as the rest of the band paused the song to mock him.

"Are you a fan?" I asked, desperately trying to act casual about it.

A small voice in the back of my head was a little concerned.

Did Nicole want to just use me to get to my friend? It wouldn't be the first time.

To be fair, it only happened one single time a few years ago, but still.

No, I scolded myself, *Nicole likes me.*

She'd been adamant about finding her own friends outside of dating me. She wouldn't use me to get to Josh. Nicole was not that kind of person.

"Yeah, I like loud heavy music like this." She giggled again as Tom, the bassist, calmly stepped forward to smack Josh on the back to help clear his airway, "I forget this guy's name, but he's lowkey my favorite. He seems like he's tolerating the rest of the guys most of the time."

I lifted an eyebrow.

She wasn't wrong.

"I think his name is Tom," I said.

Did she...not know I was friends with them?

"Tom!" She snapped her fingers, "Yes! I knew it was something basic like that. Anyway, did you know he and the drummer have been dating for years?"

I *did* know that.

Tom and Kyle were married as of last year.

Kyle dyed his hair purple for the occasion.

They both wore matching cream suits, and I might have shed a tear during Tom's heartfelt vows.

"No way." I grinned down at her, "That's so cute."

"I know. That's actually how I discovered this band, I was watching the drummer and bassist do an interview together and—" Nicole turned to look up at me again under her lashes, "Sorry. I know the manly screaming music isn't for everyone."

"Their acoustic stuff is pretty good," I shrugged under her.

"Oh, hard agree," Nicole's eyes brightened, "Wait, you listen to them, too?"

I stared at her for a moment, studying her face.

This entire conversation confused me.

Nicole *met* Josh.

At my rugby game all those weeks ago. Sure, he was wearing sunglasses and a baseball hat and a hoodie, specifically disguised to *not* be recognized by fans. But still. He had come to my games a few times before. I thought for sure word would get around about who he was.

I started mentally scanning conversations with everyone at rugby, realizing in that moment that—*oh my god*, I don't think anyone had *recognized* Josh yet.

Maybe that's why he kept bringing Susie.

His anonymity there was still alive and well.

"Taylor?" Nicole asked, adjusting so she could look at me more directly, "You okay?"

"Oh yeah," I blinked back to the present, "I listen to them. My friend got me into their music." Technically, Beck got all of us into their music.

Nicole's smile widened, "Oh my god! No way!" She shifted so that she sat up off me. I missed the feel of her warm body against mine, but watching her adjust her position so that she was on her knees next to me on the couch, excitement sparkling in her eyes, I decided to allow it. "Apparently, they haven't toured for a couple of years. But there are rumors that they might tour again in a year or so— and I've never had anyone to go to those kinds of concerts with before—"

I cut her off by placing both of my hands on her cheeks, leaning in, and kissing her.

She kissed me back, both of her hands wrapping around my wrists as she let me interrupt her excitement by brushing my lips against hers. My tongue gently tasted her plump top lip, then I nipped at the bottom one, before I leaned back and looked her in the eye.

"I'd love to go with you to their concerts."

Nicole likes Carbon Cut, so I added it to my mental Nicole jar.

Nicole's smile widened, showing all of her teeth as she happily shimmied in her seat.

"I know it's a little thing," Nicole settled, scooting closer to me again so she could wrap her arms around my shoulders, "But this is cool for me. Dating someone with my same musical tastes...planning something like that with you so far in advance..."

"To be fair, I do prefer their acoustic stuff more than his screaming songs," I brushed my nose against hers, "But I still appreciate the art. And," I kissed her more intently, trying to force my seriousness from my lips to hers, before I pulled back and said, "I like that you're planning things with me far in advance. Because I want to plan things in advance with you, too."

Nicole gently brushed my hair off my forehead before pressing a soft peck to my nose.

"Thank you," she whispered.

I lifted an eyebrow at her, "For what?"

She bit her bottom lip before smiling around it, "Just... not rolling your eyes. Or judging my interests. Making me feel safe enough to get excited about the things I like."

I frowned at her, "Girl. You should not be thanking me for that. If your partner does that to you, dump their ass."

"Well," Nicole rolled her eyes before pulling away and standing up from the couch, "Thank you for showing me what the bare minimum behavior should be, then."

I reached out to wrap my arms around her waist and pulled her down into my lap before she could step away.

"Thank you for telling me what you like," I murmured against her neck, "You are so cool."

Nicole giggled when I teased her neck with my tongue, "As long as you think I'm cool."

"And hot as hell," I spoke against her skin. I trailed my lips up her neck and nipped at her earlobe, "And fun."

Nicole sighed into my embrace, "You're fun, too. I have fun with you, no matter what we're doing."

"Good," I scraped my teeth against the shell of her ear, before dramatically tipping the two of us over on the couch, "Now hold still while I have more fun with you."

The morning shifted into laughter and moans and caresses and whispers of affection.

By the time my phone buzzed with incoming texts, an hour and a half had already passed.

I loved it.

I loved lazy mornings with Nicole.

I loved *her*.

Oddly enough, the thought wasn't terrifying at all.

It felt like a breath of fresh air to admit it to myself.

But that didn't negate the fact that this was the very first time in my adult life I had felt this way romantically toward anyone.

How did I go about proving to her that I was all in?

That, even though I had never felt the need to settle down with someone before, I was more than excited to do so now. It was a sudden shift, one I leaned into with open arms, because I knew myself well enough to know what I wanted.

What I wanted was Nicole.

Plain and simple.

I just really, really hoped she'd be open to hearing it soon.

Because I knew just how to prove it to her.

Chapter Fourteen

TAYLOR

"Good news, you're still relevant," I announced, after entering the Madey household the next day. I wanted to have a fairly serious conversation with my friends, but because of who I was as a person, I decided to ease into the conversation through good old-fashioned roasting.

All four of them, including the baby, glanced up at me from their living room seats.

"Who?" Susie asked. She and her dad were sitting on opposite sides of the coffee table, putting together a massive jigsaw puzzle. Courtney sat on the couch with baby boy Cooper on her lap. He immediately resumed gnawing on his teething ring.

"Your father." I nodded toward Josh, who raised his dark brows at me with a smirk. Adjusting the glasses on his nose, he chuckled and focused on the puzzle.

"I'll bite. Why am I still relevant?" Josh asked.

"Because Nicole is into your music." I plopped myself down in one of the ugly accent chairs, watching them continue piecing together the outer exterior of the puzzle. "And I'm pretty sure she has no idea she's met you already."

"At rugby?" Courtney asked. Cooper randomly chucked the teething toy across the couch, then laughed when his mom had to reach across to retrieve it for him.

"Yup."

"You don't think she knows who I am?" Josh asked. He frowned at a puzzle piece in his hand before Susie plucked it from his fingertips and placed it in a spot closer to her.

"No, because after your music started playing, she looked at me and apologized."

"Why?" Susie asked.

"It was your dad's older stuff. From before you were born," I explained, "He screamed a lot. She assumed I didn't like it."

"But...you don't like it." Susie cocked her head at me.

"The point is," I leaned forward, resting my elbows on my knees and clasping my hands together, "While I was sitting there wondering if she was playing the music because she knew I was friends with you, it became very apparent that she has *no idea* that I'm friends with you. And she clocked me as someone who doesn't like heavier music like that."

"You don't," Susie said again.

"Oh my god," I rolled my eyes at the stinker, "Fine. It's not my first choice. But it's clearly Nicole's. And she has no idea how close she is to a band she enjoys listening to."

"So, what makes you bring this up?" Courtney asked. Cooper was wearing a bib around his neck to catch the drool, and Courtney lifted the bib to dab at his cheeks and lips.

"I thought it might be nice to, I don't know..." I scratched the back of my head. "Maybe have you sign something for her. Formally meet her, or something." I shrugged, lowering my hand so I could rub both of them together.

Silence greeted me after my words.

I glanced up to see Court and Josh sharing a look before they both turned to me. Susie was focused on her puzzle, and Cooper was busy gnawing on his teether.

"But, why?" Josh pressed, grinning when he finally placed a puzzle piece in the right spot.

"Why not?" I countered, leaning back in my chair and crossing my arms, "It's not like you're busy."

"Heaven forbid I enjoy a few years off from touring," Josh snickered as Susie plucked his next piece from his hand and added it to her side of the puzzle again.

"But meeting Nicole and signing something for her would take two seconds out of your day," I countered.

"But why, T?" Courtney pressed. I glanced up at her, ready to repeat myself, before she interrupted me, "I know, logically there's no issue with this request. But *why* do you want to do this for Nicole? She's not the first person you've dated who likes Carbon Cut's music. She won't be the last. You've never felt the need to show Josh off for relationship points before. So, why now?"

I opened and closed my mouth a couple of times before releasing a heavy sigh and scraping a hand down my face.

"What if...Nicole *was* the last person I dated?" I finally asked.

I had to give it to Court, because she didn't get silly or teasing. She thoughtfully studied me. My words lingered thick in the air, and the more I let them soak into the moment, the safer the admission felt.

However, I stood, scraping my hands over my face as I started to pace back and forth. My friends knew me as the chronically single friend. The one who always left the party early to go hook up with someone. Hell, Beck and I bonded over never wanting to get married at Josh and Courtney's wedding.

So, I essentially threw my closest friends a sudden curveball.

"Taylor Desmond," Courtney's voice was quieter. When I glanced over at her, I realized that the reason for her softer tone was that Cooper's eyes were starting to droop with sleepiness. "Are you...really that into Nicole?"

Susie glanced up from her puzzle with a frown on her face. "Why is this bad?"

I didn't know how to answer that, so I let Josh answer for me.

"It's not bad at all," Josh explained to his daughter, "But Taylor doesn't usually settle down with one specific person."

"...Right. They're polyamorous," Susie stated. This nine-year-old had a healthier understanding of the different types of romantic relationship dynamics than most adults. Then Susie looked at me, "Is Nicole?"

"I'm not polyamorous. More like, ethically non-monogamous. Never wanted to settle down—until now, that is." I huffed a laugh at that, running my fingers through my hair, "Nicole is the settle-down type."

"The reason this surprises your mom and me," Josh continued to explain to Susie, "Is that in the past, when Taylor found a monogamous person that they wanted to date, they agreed that they would be monogamous until Taylor formed a crush on someone else. When that happened, Taylor would let them know, and their relationship would end. Now, Taylor is saying they *just* want to be with Nicole. That they don't want to form a crush on someone else."

Susie nodded. "...Okay." Then she focused back on her puzzle. Josh and Courtney struggled not to laugh at the clear dismissal. How this revelation was such a non-issue in her mind. I shrugged and plopped back down in the chair.

"So. That's what's new with me," I shrugged with my words, "What's new with—"

"When did you decide this, T?" Courtney interrupted me while gently brushing her son's hair back away from his face. Josh gave me a quick glance before focusing back on the puzzle with his daughter.

"I don't know if it was one specific moment, if I'm being honest," I shrugged, before plopping down on the floor to join in on the puzzle. "My feelings for her both snuck up on me and have been very present the whole time. It's hard to explain."

Courtney nodded, "Do you love her?"

At that, Susie lifted her eyes to meet mine, "Ooooo."

I smiled, before looking back at Courtney and replying with a simple, "Yes...and it's a little terrifying. But mostly exciting."

"Damn," Josh whistled with a single shake of his head, "Taylor Desmond is in love. I never thought I'd see the day."

"Wow," I deadpanned, "Be more surprised, please."

"Are you going to marry her?" Susie asked.

I puffed my cheeks with air, before dramatically exhaling it and shaking my head, "I don't know. She wants to get married someday, so probably."

"And you're cool with that?" Josh asked as he quirked his lips at his puzzle piece.

I plucked it from his fingers, before handing it to Susie.

She immediately placed it in the proper spot.

"Yeah," I found myself smiling at the thought of Nicole walking down an aisle toward me. Would she wear a white dress? Champagne? A suit? "Yeah, I'm cool with that."

"I want to get married someday, too," Susie chimed in. "How are you going to propose to Nicole?"

I tucked my lips between my teeth, narrowing my eyes at Susie Madey.

"That probably won't happen for a while. First, I want to exploit your dad's fame to win some extra points with her." It was more than that, though, "Then, I want to tell her I love her."

I rarely, if ever, introduced my partners to Courtney and Josh. Beck and Adam, sure. Even Logan and Eloise, on occasion, unless they were super into hockey and remembered Logan from his time in the NHL.

But this was different.

Because Nicole was different.

I wanted her to be part of my circles, even if she was scared to insert herself into them.

For years, I had seen my friends in loving, lasting partnerships. They found one person and established a life with them. Some got married; some had kids. Beck and Adam did neither of those things but still had a stronger, safer relationship than most married people I knew.

"I just want to give this a real chance," I nodded, "Nicole is the first person I've had these big feelings for." I stretched my back out before adjusting my seat on the floor. "I want to show Nicole that I'm ready to commit to her, if she feels the same way I do."

"Not just hold her hand and kiss her?" Susie pressed with a raised blonde eyebrow.

"I mean, obviously holding hands and kissing will happen too." I winked at her before she rolled her eyes and focused back on the puzzle with her dad and me.

Mumbling to herself, Susie muttered, "Kissing is so *gross*. There are so many germs in our mouths. Dad and I did an experiment where we swabbed the inside of our cheeks and grew the bacteria from them inside a petri dish." Susie shuddered, emphasizing her disgust.

"You're not wrong about the germs," Josh squinted at the puzzle, pushing his glasses up his nose, "But kissing can be pretty great with the right person." He gave Courtney a loving glance over his daughter's head.

Susie shook her head and made a grossed-out face, "Pass."

Josh lifted a shoulder, "Suit yourself." Josh turned to me, "T, How can I help you woo your woman?"

I smirked at the world-famous rockstar, "We shouldn't make a big deal out of it. Let me tell you my idea."

Chapter Fifteen

NICOLE

A WEEK after Taylor told Violet we were having sleepovers, Leo, Jacqueline, Signe, Zaid, and I were all walking into the building together. Leo pushed against the door, which didn't budge.

As he stepped back to examine it, his dark brows pinched in confusion.

So, I informed him, "It's a pull."

Leo immediately hit me with, "Oi! Cheers, love, my next plan was to start lifting from the bottom but thank god you were here to tell me to pull."

Signe threw her head back before releasing a loud laugh.

Zaid lowered his face to chuckle as he grabbed her hand and led her through the threshold.

"How many times have you walked through this door? Why did you magically think it would turn into a push?" I asked Leo before stepping into our building. He and Jacqueline followed in after me.

"I didn't get a lot of sleep last night," Leo replied, throwing Jacqueline a wink.

She lifted a dark eyebrow at him before giving me a bored look, "He stayed up on his phone watching this animated rock opera series he discovered on YouTube. I took his phone away when I woke up at 3:00 am to see he hadn't gone to sleep yet."

I snickered as we all piled into the elevator together to take us to Sun Steer's floor.

"Is my replacement being interviewed today?" Signe asked after a moment of silence.

"I hope so," Jacqueline replied.

Signe dropped her jaw, widening her eyes at Jacqueline in offense, "What the hell does that mean?"

Jacqueline pinched her eyebrows together in confusion before clarity hit, and she panicked, "Wait, no! I didn't mean it like that. I just meant I'm tired of interviewing people—I'm so sorry."

Signe, the big teddy bear she was, laughed and squeezed Jacqueline in a side hug, "I'm just teasing you."

Jacqueline's shoulders visibly dropped at the reassurance. Leo rested his hand on her lower back until the elevator doors opened, and we all stepped off.

"Oh! You're here." Jacqueline stepped ahead of all of us and reached a hand toward a stranger loitering in front of Signe's desk.

Brandon Moore was also standing in front of Signe's desk, a visible frown on his face as he stared down at the woman who must have been one of Jacqueline's interviewees. She wore light-wash jeans and sneakers, with a white button-up shirt French-tucked into the front. She was curvaceous, with a soft, feminine body that resembled my own.

"Hi. I'm Nora," The woman turned to give Brandon her

shoulder as she shook Jacqueline's hand, "I know I'm a little early. I can wait for you to get settled if you need."

"No need," Jacqueline nodded her head in the direction of her office, "You're my only interview today." Nora grinned before flicking her dark eyes dismissively at Brandon. She tucked her honey-blonde hair behind her ears, showing off multiple cartilage piercings, and followed Jacqueline and Leo.

When she gave us her back, I noticed that underneath her hair was dyed a dark pink.

"Good luck!" Signe gave Nora two thumbs up as she set her bag on her desk.

Zaid pecked Signe on the head before he walked toward the software engineer's wing of the building.

Brandon, however, looked stuck. He was still staring after Nora as she and Jacqueline rounded the corner toward upper management's offices.

"Hey," I elbowed Brandon to pull his attention away from her, "What's your deal?"

Brandon blushed.

It wasn't a subtle one either, but a dark one. His entire face turned bright red.

"I think I messed up." he released a heavy sigh as he fell into step with me, heading toward our own offices. "Nora is a barista at the coffee shop I frequent. This morning, I might have snapped at her for getting my drink wrong." He pinched the bridge of his nose between his fingers.

Brandon didn't know it, but something opened in my chest at the admission from him. This wasn't a casual conversation between two coworkers anymore. With a couple of sentences, I realized that Brandon possibly considered me to be, to some degree at least, a friend.

No man would ever bring something like this up with a

coworker, let alone a female coworker. This was something you'd bring up with someone you trusted and respected. Someone you felt relatively safe with.

It hit me then.

Brandon and I were *friends*.

And as a friend, he was gently reaching out for advice.

"Oh," I held in a laugh because Brandon didn't seem to think this situation was funny, "Well, she might not take the job now that she knows you own the place."

Brandon frowned at that, "Which will make Jacqueline's team have to look for someone else to fill Signe's position. Again."

I lifted a shoulder in silent agreement before saying, "Or you could try to catch her on her way out. After Jacqueline's interview, I mean. Apologize. Make sure she knows you won't be rude to her if she's hired."

Brandon nodded at that, "You don't think that would make it worse?"

I shook my head, "As long as you keep your apology brief and to the point, I think you'll be fine. You don't come off as someone who harasses people."

"Oh, thank god," Brandon looked genuinely relieved as he sighed his response. We made it to our offices, right next to each other, before he nodded at me, "Thanks."

"You're welcome." I smiled before unlocking my door and stepping through the threshold.

As soon as I took my phone out of my bag and set it on my desk, it vibrated.

> Taylor: Are you coming to rugby tonight? I want to formally introduce you to my friends.

That made me pause.

It'd been a while since our first date, when I explained my fears.

My fears about having mutual friends.

My fears about their friends, possibly, becoming my friends.

My fears about feeling abandoned if Taylor and I didn't end up working out long-term.

But I sat with those feelings, resting my phone on my desk to breathe through it.

I couldn't hide from their friends forever. If I wanted something long-term, I needed to be part of their life, too.

When I heard Brandon answer a call through the thin wall we shared between our offices, I jerked my head up, recalling the conversation he and I had just had, and the revelation I had with it.

That was what I wanted, wasn't it? Friends? Community? People I could lean on, and people who could lean on me in return? I mean, even Jacqueline and Leo were good friends of mine. Signe, too. Zaid was a little more shy, but I had a feeling that if I had a flat tire and everyone else was busy, he would come help me change it without hesitation.

Warmth filled my chest at the thought.

I recalled Leo giving me shit when I teased him about opening the door to our building wrong.

Signe, Violet, Jacqueline, Mary, and Jamie, all hanging out at Signe's apartment after work. Clad in jammies.

My relationship with Taylor wasn't a *threat* to any of that.

They were an *addition* to all of my friendships.

It hit me then.

It caught me off guard. It happened so naturally.

I had friendships. Mine. Just because Leo and Jacqueline also happened to be friends with Taylor, it didn't mean that they weren't also *my* friends. In my corner. Both could be true. The trauma of my past relationship made me want to draw all these clear lines in the sand, keeping my social circles perfectly organized so that if a hypothetical situation did arise, I'd be as protected as possible.

But...I was just holding myself back this whole time.

And Taylor was being so patient with me, too.

Even via text. They were giving me a chance to say I was busy with work by warning me what their intention was. To meet their friends.

I didn't want to keep holding myself back. I couldn't keep doing things scared. I needed to start doing things with a glass-half-full perspective.

So, I picked my phone up and replied to my partner.

> Me: I can if you want me to.

> Taylor: Obviously, I want you to.

I smiled, embracing the warm flutter in my stomach while reading their text.

> Me: Then, obviously, I'll be there.

The next text that came in was a picture of Taylor.

Their hair had grown long enough for them to tie into a ponytail on the back of their head, showing off their fresh fade. They were standing in their office at the clinic, giving the camera a silly smile with flexed nostrils and crazy eyebrows.

I barked a laugh before covering my mouth to smother the sound.

They were so unserious.

I glanced around my office before sitting in my desk chair and sending back a normal selfie. I angled my head to show off my good side. I kept the phone camera just below eye level, instead of high above my head like I used to do as a teenager. I smiled widely, letting my eyes crinkle a bit to show how their picture made me laugh.

I sent it.

They heart-reacted to it almost immediately.

> Taylor: I love your smile lines.

My heart thumped in my chest.

Taylor Desmond had mastered the art of compliments. They gave them to me freely. As soon as the thought entered their head, they said it. I wasn't used to it.

I loved it.

> Me: I love getting your goofy selfies.

> Taylor: Thank god. See you tonight, babe.

I sighed before setting my phone down and forcing myself to lock in for the rest of the day. I was experiencing the honeymoon phase with them. I was falling, quickly.

On paper, it all seemed way too fast.

But I didn't want to care about that.

Taylor was *wonderful*.

I felt safe with them. I felt appreciated. I felt *wanted*. When was the last time I felt all of this with a partner? Consistently like this?

They knew my concerns about breaking up with mutual friends.

If they were going out of their way to "formally" introduce me to their friends tonight, that meant something to them. They knew that meant something to me.

They were acting like they were *all* in.

Like they didn't *want* to break up.

Ever.

Perhaps it was time for me to have a chat with them again. We hadn't talked about the progress of our relationship in detail since that conversation during our date.

Perhaps this was a new, improved Nicole.

Willing to take what she wants.

Done mourning her last breakup.

Ready to step into the deep end with someone she did not expect at all.

"Yeah," I sighed to myself as I clicked my laptop to life, "Tonight, we'll talk."

I tried really hard not to think myself into a negative, anxious spiral about my plans for the rest of the day. Before, it would be easy for me to focus on the risk of getting too close to Taylor and their friends. We already had a couple of mutual friends, my coworkers, whom I cherished more and more every day.

I didn't want to lose them if things went south with Taylor and me.

But I didn't want my fears and insecurities to get in the way of this, either.

There was a chance all of this would work out, right?

That Taylor and I could be happy together.

They wouldn't want me to meet their friends if they didn't think that, too.

So instead of worrying about sharing my friends with them at their rugby practice today, I forced myself to get lost in numbers, budgets, and company spending.

I'd found success in my career, but for some reason, finding success with romance felt much more intimidating.

Chapter Sixteen

NICOLE

Taylor: You coming?

Me: I'm just finishing up work.

Taylor: Can't wait to see you!

I GRINNED to myself as I saved my work and closed my laptop. I decided to run home and change, considering I had a bit of time before rugby practice was supposed to start. I reapplied deodorant, added some blush to my cheeks, and applied a coat of mascara. I was getting dolled up to watch Taylor at their rugby practice.

It wasn't even a date.

It was just Taylor.

Leo and Zaid would be there. Maybe Jacqueline and Signe, depending on how her morning-but-actually-all-day sickness was going.

This would be the first time Taylor and I hung out with our mutual friends since we became, well, *us*.

Would they want me to kiss them hello?

Would they hold me like they have so many nights now?

150

I wasn't sure. But I was excited to find out. I mean, they *asked* for me to come. Surely that meant that they were excited for me to be there? That they wanted their current partner to sit with everyone? Their friends?

I drove over to the field, remembering to bring a flannel cover-up to protect me against the marine layer rolling in from the ocean.

My shorts and sneakers would cool me off if it didn't get as cold as expected.

As I strolled down the pathway from the parking lot to the grass where Taylor and their team were already practicing, I saw a person waving.

It was the tattooed dad from weeks ago.

One of Taylor's friends.

Still wearing his sunglasses and hoodie with the hood on.

He was sitting on a picnic blanket with his blonde-haired daughter. The one who made him pay her for swearing. I waved back, intending to find my spot to sit, when I realized Jacqueline and Signe were sitting on a blanket beside them, deep in discussion.

The dad and daughter were staring at me, and even though their expressions were polite and not leering, it made my nerves erupt in my gut.

Was this guy married? Did he have a partner? Was he staring at me because he liked what he saw?

One of my least favorite things in the world was explaining to men that I was very, very gay. Most men didn't handle the rejection well.

Because they were men.

But he was friends with Taylor, and they wouldn't be friends with bad men.

I quietly avoided eye contact and made my way over to

Signe and Jacqueline. When I did, the tattooed dad and daughter started whispering to each other.

"Hi," I greeted my coworkers.

"Oh! What are you doing here?" Signe asked, scooting over to make room for me. She even went as far as to cover me with some of the blanket she held on her lap. I happily snuggled in.

"I came to watch Taylor," I replied.

Jacqueline turned to look at me, her dark eyes studying my face with that quiet intensity she was known for.

"What?" I asked her.

"Can we talk about you two now?" Jacqueline asked.

Signe dramatically leaned forward to catch my eye, and her dark red eyebrows practically disappeared into her hairline. "Talk about what?"

"Um—" I was cut off when the visual of the team running near our side of the field caught my eye. Taylor was ahead of the team. Their frame was much smaller than the men they played with. Taylor didn't need to wear a sports bra, but they had one on underneath their oversized cutoff t-shirt anyway. It showed off the entirety of their waist and the lean definition of their muscles and back. One wrong breeze, and their top could expose their entire front. The plain black sports bra made more sense to me now.

When Taylor jogged by, glancing to the side to see me sitting between Jacqueline and Signe, they comedically skidded to a stop and backpedaled to stand in front of me.

Their smile stretched across their face, showing off all their teeth. Fine smile lines formed in the crinkles of their eyes, and they quickly scratched their septum piercing before stepping toward us.

"She's here, T!" the blonde little girl called over. Her dad grinned before elbowing his daughter's ribs and lifting his index finger to his mouth to shush her.

"Damn, be cool, Susie," Taylor replied with a wink. Then they turned to me again, before crouching in front of our blanket, "Practice just started, and I only ran one lap so far."

I glanced at Jacqueline and Signe just to double-check, but the way Taylor locked their eyes on me confirmed that they were talking to me, specifically.

"...Okay." I felt heat stain my cheeks from their direct attention, my heart fluttering in my chest when they smirked at my response.

"What I'm saying is, I'm not sweaty and gross yet," Taylor raised a dark eyebrow, and then their eyes lowered a fraction. They were still staring at me, or more accurately, my mouth. When their tongue darted out to moisten their bottom lip, I suspected their intention.

But...I wasn't sure. So, I shifted forward a bit, lowering the blanket Signe shared with me just a fraction as I asked, "Um—do you, uh—" I glanced at my coworkers again.

Signe was staring wide-eyed at the two of us with the largest shit-eating grin on her face. Jacqueline was giving me a much more normal smile as she watched this interaction between Taylor and me.

"Nicole," Taylor shifted forward toward me, letting their knees hit the grass as their hands supported their weight on the picnic blanket. Their dark hair fell onto their forehead, so they brushed it out of their eyes as they said, "I want to kiss the shit out of you."

My heart felt like it was beating too fast. I was getting so dizzy from their direct attention. Their baggy cutoff shirt fell loose in front of them, giving me a perfect view of their sports bra and their toned stomach.

They were too much.

I couldn't think straight.

"Pay up!" the little girl called from the side.

"Not this time, Suse," her dad murmured.

Taylor gave the little girl some playful side-eye before crawling toward me once more.

"Okay—" and that's all I got out before they pounced on me.

They *literally* pounced on me. They pushed me down on Signe's picnic blanket, grasped both of my cheeks, and attacked my lips with their own. Their septum piercing was cool against my lips and cheeks. They kept giving me smacking, drugging kisses again and again.

I was vaguely aware of Signe next to us, squealing with excitement and whistling.

Their thigh was between both of mine, through the blanket, and heat pooled inside me immediately.

Laughter erupted out of me whenever Taylor gave me a chance to breathe.

It was so...*Taylor*.

Immediately easing any spiraling concerns on how to play this out. For them to stop what they were doing and pepper kisses all over my face as soon as they saw me, not a care in the world if our mutual friends were around to see us.

I finally managed, after processing my surprise, to wrap both of my arms around their shoulders and kiss them back. They grinned against my lips, letting me try to be as aggressive as they were with me.

After Signe's cheers and heckling quieted down, Taylor finally pulled away from me just enough to sigh, "That's better," against my lips.

I giggled, like a lovesick schoolgirl, "Hi."

"Hello, babe." Taylor brushed their nose with mine. Then gave my nose a quick peck of a kiss.

"Where's T?" An unfamiliar woman's voice asked.

"Being gross," the little girl answered her.

"Grow up," her dad replied.

"I'm nine," she rebutted.

I laughed at the exchange before Taylor finally pushed off me and grasped my hands to pull me back into my sitting position. Kneeling in front of me, they glanced at the tattooed dad next to us.

"Can I introduce you to my friends?" Taylor asked me.

At that, Jacqueline scooted back on the blanket, getting out of the way so Taylor could introduce me to the dad and daughter, and a blonde woman who looked like the grown-up version of the little girl. The woman held a baby, comfortably wrapped in a blanket. The baby even wore a little beanie to cover their ears and protect them from the cool weather.

After briefly studying the four of them, I realized they must be a family.

"Nicole, these are some of my best friends," Taylor gestured toward the woman, "This is Courtney."

"Nice to meet you." The blonde woman adjusted the baby on her lap, sitting cross-legged, and held a hand toward me to shake.

"Nice to meet you, too." I noticed an oddly shaped birthmark on the top of her hand, which felt familiar to me for some reason. Perhaps she and I had already met before?

"This is their daughter, Susie," Taylor continued with introductions.

"Hi!" The little girl shuffled forward and threw both of her arms around my shoulders. She squeezed me tight as she spoke against my shoulder, "I'm so excited to finally meet you—even if you and T grossed me out."

I laughed, before wrapping my arms around her little waist, "I'm so sorry about that."

"I'm not." Taylor laughed.

Susie pulled back and looked at my face for a moment. A dimpled grin appeared on her cheeks.

"T was right. You're really pretty." She nodded once and looked over at Taylor, "Good job."

Taylor snorted, "Thanks," and gently shoved Susie off me. The nine-year-old smiled mischievously as she started darting her gaze between her dad and me.

"And this," Taylor scooted toward me, lowering their voice just a hair, as if they were letting me in on a secret, "Is Courtney's husband, Josh."

"Hello." Josh reached forward and wrapped his much larger, fully tattooed hand in mine. It was a brief handshake, which I was grateful for. I was picking up on Susie's excitement over meeting her dad, but I couldn't figure out why.

I barely glanced up at his sunglasses before muttering, "Hi." To him.

"...Madey," Taylor added, after Josh released my hand.

Madey?

"Oh!" I turned toward Taylor with a smile at the coincidence, "Like Joshua Madey? That's crazy! That's just like—" I gasped after I turned back to face Josh, who had removed his sunglasses and pulled his hood down.

"Oh my god," Signe muttered behind me.

"Well," Josh lifted a shoulder while combing through his dark brown hair with his fingers, "Your girl definitely didn't know who I was, T."

Oh my god, I'm Taylor's girl.

I just stared at him.

Frozen in shock, partially because I had just casually been introduced to the lead singer of Carbon Cut, and partially because the lead singer of Carbon Cut referred to me as *Taylor's* girl. That meant that Taylor had talked to him about our relationship. Positively, because no one would refer to me as their girl unless they *wanted* to claim me as their girl.

I also hadn't *met* a celebrity before.

I had seen random celebrities growing up in southern California, but usually, it was the celebrities I wasn't excited about. The ones my friends were excited to meet. Not one I was a big fan of myself.

I silently reached over and clasped Taylor's hand in mine.

Josh tilted his head back and laughed at the movement, while his wife—which I now realized was Courtney motherfucking Henderson, the woman Josh pulled onto his stage years and years ago—grinned at me.

"I'm sorry." What was I apologizing for? I had no idea, "Just. Wow."

"Hey, babe, breathe." Taylor kissed my cheek right when Leo called out to them from the field.

"Oi!" He was cupping his hands around his mouth to amplify the sound, "We need our captain to start training!"

"Get off my dick!" Taylor called back.

"Don't have too much fun without me. I'll be back." Their fingers trailed up my back, skimmed up my neck, and cupped the back of my head before tipping me back to gently brush their lips over mine.

"They just said dick; do they owe you money for that?" I heard Signe ask Susie from behind us.

"Dick isn't a bad word. It's a body part." Susie replied.

"Don't forget about me, okay?" Taylor murmured against my lips.

I scoffed, right in their face, making them jolt away from me in amusement.

"Never," I whispered.

Taylor grinned, a rosy pink that wasn't there before appeared across their cheeks, before they finally stood up and jogged back to their teammates.

When I looked back at Josh, he was pulling his hoodie up again.

"Did you like your surprise?" Susie asked me. She was sitting cross-legged, but excited energy made her bounce in her seat.

"Yeah," I replied, glancing behind me. At some point, Jacqueline had scooted far enough back to sit closer to Signe. I gave the two of them wide-eyed looks. Signe was grinning, and Jacqueline had her eyebrows raised.

"Wow, so," I cleared my throat before turning to face the Madeys. The *Madeys*. Not only did I just meet the lead singer of Carbon Cut, but I also met his entire family.

Wow.

"So," Susie giggled.

"You're friends with Taylor," I added.

"To be clear, I was friends with them first," Courtney leaned forward, as if to remind me that she was also there. I grinned at her, connecting the dots. Courtney became famous because she interpreted Josh's concert into ASL for her friend, and he noticed her. Apparently, they were high school sweethearts, reconnecting after almost a decade apart. I glanced at the birthmark on top of her hand again, realizing why it looked so familiar.

That birthmark was how Josh knew who she was.

"Really?" I asked her. If memory served, Courtney had

been involved in lots of charity work recently. I admired this woman a lot.

"Yeah, and then I married Josh."

"And I was invited into the circle of friendship." Josh grinned at his wife before taking their baby boy from her and adjusting him so he could face out toward the field. The baby grinned and started wiggling in his father's hold, as if trying to get to the rugby players.

"What a small world," I breathed. Taylor ran by, yelling at Zaid around the mouth guard they wore, and I got distracted watching them take a man almost double their size down to the grass.

I had seen them play before, and even though they were one of the smallest members on the team, they were strong.

Leo and Zaid immediately jogged over and helped Taylor to their feet, who dusted their jersey off before clapping their hands and telling their team to start whatever drill that was again.

"Nicole?" Susie's voice pulled me back into the present: "Do you want to plan a future with Taylor, or do you just want to hold their hand and kiss them?"

Josh's eyebrows shot up as Courtney leaned forward to rest a hand on her daughter's shoulder and say, "Suse, that's too forward of a question to ask someone you just met."

I giggled, appreciating Josh and Courtney's embarrassment.

"That's okay," I reassured them before addressing their daughter, "I really like Taylor."

"We do, too," Susie replied, "...but I don't want to kiss them."

"Well, that's fine," I replied, nudging her knee with my fist, "I like that I'm the only one who gets to kiss them."

Susie grinned up at me, before her gaze dropped to my arm and she pointed at it, "Can I see your tattoo?"

"Sure." My flannel had ridden up my arm, so she got a peek of the latest one I got. It was still covered in saniderm, since I got it two nights before on an impulse decision. It was simple, a daisy right on the inside of my wrist. I decided to remove my flannel from that arm completely so Susie could admire the random patchwork tattoos I had on my upper arm, too.

"I like this one," She pointed to the tattoo of a raccoon, holding a bouquet of flowers.

"I do, too."

"Does this have a special meaning?" Susie asked. I shrugged.

"It means the drawing was cute and I wanted it on my body forever."

"So can I copy it?" Susie asked me.

I laughed at her question before replying, "Um, sure."

At that, Susie reached into her school bag she had with her and pulled out a pen, before holding it out to her dad. Josh sighed, handing the baby back to Courtney, before uncapping the pen and getting to work on his daughter's request. She held her arm out for him while smiling up at me.

Joshua Madey is drawing my tattoo on his daughter's arm.

"Oh my god, wait—" Courtney sat up straighter, looking intently over my shoulder, "Are you Signe Lange?"

"Stop it," Signe replied, "*You* know who *I* am?"

"I'm obsessed with your book!" Courtney lit up, adjusting her baby in her lap, "You're friends with Eloise St. James, right? She told me to read your book, and I'm *so* glad I did!"

"Wait, really?" Josh glanced up from his drawing, "What's the title?"

"Stop it right now!" Signe exclaimed. I looked over my shoulder, keeping my arm visible for Josh to view for reference, and saw Signe tugging at the collar of her sweater and hiding her face behind it.

Jacqueline and I shared a laugh, and the rest of the evening settled in like that. Me, geeking out over a famous musician drawing my tattoo on his daughter. His wife, Courtney, geeking out over meeting Signe Lange, her new favorite romance author.

Taylor checked in every few minutes as they took a water break, smiling brightly at the sight of all of us mingling. I tried to see it through their eyes, how it would feel to have everyone from different worlds come together. To support them like this.

This was *big*, I realized.

They weren't just introducing me to their friends; they were introducing me to a very vulnerable friendship. They were *trusting* me with the knowledge of *who* they were friends with.

Taylor felt safe sharing their people with me.

Something warm bloomed in my chest, and I found myself slightly less interested in the rockstar beside me and more interested in my partner running around on the field, outdoing so many men on their team with their speed.

I needed to tell them tonight.

Surprisingly, I wasn't scared to.

In fact, I was really looking forward to it.

Chapter Seventeen

TAYLOR

NICOLE and I walked into my apartment together later that night. We weren't as chatty as we normally were, but I decided to give her some grace, considering who she just met today.

"Are you doing all right?" I asked, resting a hand on her back as she slid her sneakers off.

"Yeah, yeah." She shook her head, before a giggle escaped her lips, "Oh my god. I just met Joshua Madey from Carbon Cut."

"And his wife and kids," I added, delighted that she was thrilled about the surprise.

"I just—," Nicole's dark eyes widened at me, "I feel so honored."

I raised an eyebrow at her, "Honored?"

"Yeah." She set her bag on the ground and stepped toward me. I was sweaty and disgusting, with a few grass stains on my shorts and knees. "You shared some special people with me."

I lifted a shoulder, my heart fluttering at her acknowledgement.

I'm trying to show you, I thought, *I want you. All of you. Be with me.*

"I wanted those people to meet someone special, actually." I tucked a strand of her black hair behind her ear, loving the goosebumps that erupted on her neck from my fingertips. I let my hand rest on the part of her neck that met her shoulder, gently dragging my thumb across her pulse point in gentle swipes.

"You have a lot of reasons to be hesitant about us," I gestured between the two of us for emphasis, "But I'm happy to keep giving you reasons to give us a real chance."

"Taylor?" Nicole whispered.

"Hmm?"

"I'm in love with you."

I froze at her quiet words.

Was that the first time I had ever heard those words? No. Not at all. I've had people in my past tell me they were falling in love with me, and unfortunately, my feelings simply weren't reciprocated.

Perhaps that's what made this time so different.

Instead of panic, anxiety, and a hint of sadness that usually came with me having to start the "It's not you, it's me" cliché, I felt something unfamiliar but fantastic.

Excitement.

Satisfaction.

Hope.

Love.

"That's good," I smirked down at her, loving how vulnerable she looked. How she waited so patiently for me to respond, gnawing on her bottom lip as she did so, "Because I think I've been in love with you since the beginning."

Nicole's eyes widened, before a shocked huff of a laugh erupted from her lips.

"The beginning?" She raised a dark eyebrow at me in disbelief, but she still stepped closer to me. She ignored how sweaty and smelly I was, resting her forearms on my chest as I wrapped one of mine around her waist.

"Since the moment I saw you at Signe's apartment."

Nicole's brows furrowed, before her brow smoothed, and she shook her head, "When Signe's friend showed up to get her book signed? You—you saw me there?"

"Yeah." I stepped toward my bedroom, guiding her backward through my apartment, "I gave Jacqueline a hug, accidentally spilled the beans that she was boinking Leo, and turned around to see you." I released my hold on her waist to flick the light on in my bedroom. "It was the first time my heart skipped a beat on sight."

"On sight?" Nicole asked with a shake of her head.

"Yes." I laughed at her surprise, "You were so cute, in your little matching jammies. Yellow, with flowers all over them. I wanted to invite myself to stay, but I knew Eloise and Courtney would give me shit for bailing on them."

Nicole nodded, "Wow. You couldn't have been in love with me in that moment, though."

I shrugged, stepping back and pulling my shirt off. My sports bra remained, and Nicole's dark eyes darkened even more as she stared at my stomach, "Maybe not. But something deep in my soul recognized you. That, I do not doubt. When I saw you again at rugby, when Jacqueline performed her little dance, I wanted to talk to you again. But I choked."

"I can't believe this," Nicole blushed when I pushed my pants down. I wasn't wearing anything sexy. My underwear was athletic and resembled boxers more than anything else.

But Nicole liked what she saw. Her poker face was non-existent.

"Well," I lifted a shoulder, "Believe it. I love you."

Nicole sucked in a sharp breath. This time, my words looked like they solidified something in her, instead of surprising her, "I love you, too."

"Well," I clapped my hands together, "That's settled."

Nicole barked a laugh, "Wow," she plopped herself on the edge of my bed, "Go shower, babe."

"Join me?" I asked, sliding my underwear down my legs.

Nicole's jaw slackened as her eyes watched the material descend from my legs.

"Okay." With that, she stood up and pulled her shirt off, "I guess you're allowed to clean up before I can taste you."

It was my turn to blush.

Would she ever stop triggering such a visceral reaction in me?

Probably not.

Nicole confidently disrobed before taking my hand and letting me lead her into the shower.

Love was so *freeing*.

Nicole's love was *safe*.

As we settled under the warm spray, we spent time gently washing the day off of us. Reverently cleansing each other in a way that I wasn't used to experiencing with a partner. As if we were getting ready to start a new normal.

Maybe that was exactly it.

A new era.

One where I could run home and find comfort in Nicole's embrace every night.

An era where we could be each other's person, however we needed.

A relationship that we could rely on. That was built on trust and comfort and respect and, most importantly, love.

After the shower, Nicole gently pushed my shoulders until I fell flat on my back, on top of the comforter. In that moment, I told her that I felt like the luckiest person alive.

Nicole kept murmuring how much she loved me.

Each kiss, each touch, each caress felt like solidification. We showed each other with our bodies just how much we cared for the other. How much we wanted to be *here*. How much we *appreciated* being here, in this beautiful moment.

After finding bliss in each other, we snuggled in for the night. Still naked, vulnerable, and satiated. I rested my chin on top of her head as I held her chest to chest.

"I love you," I whispered through a yawn.

"I love you, too," Nicole whispered back.

Within seconds, I succumbed to the best sleep of my entire life.

Chapter Eighteen

TAYLOR

"THANKS AGAIN FOR COMING," I said, squeezing Nicole's hand with mine.

"Of course," she smiled at me, squeezing my hand back.

Today, I was introducing her to one of my favorite people ever.

Beck's grandmother. Susie's namesake.

As we strolled through the cemetery in Laguna Hills, our voices lowered. Nicole's demeanor immediately shifted to reverent and respectful. I tried to hide a smirk at the thought that, had Susan still been alive, she'd hate that.

She'd want Nicole to act like herself.

To have *fun*.

"I'm excited to meet more of your friends," Nicole murmured, studying all the gravestones we passed on the way to Susan's. At first, I felt worried that I was introducing Nicole to too many people. Here I was, showing off this massive support system of friends I considered family, whereas Nicole's support system was much smaller. The friends she claimed as her own, I already knew.

It felt one-sided.

But Nicole reassured me that she was fine, even if it was a bit overwhelming for her at the beginning.

"Me too," I grinned down at her, "Beck is one of my favorite people. Adam is great, too. Once he opens up."

Nicole hummed as we strolled hand in hand, before Beck and Adam came into view. They had already set up a picnic blanket in front of Susan's grave, snacks were distributed, and when Adam nudged Beck to inform her of our arrival, she beamed and waved dramatically at us.

"Beck is hard of hearing," I informed Nicole, "Even though she's wearing hearing aids, it's best to let her get a view of your face when you speak to her. That way, she can read your lips, too."

"Got it," Nicole nodded.

Adam and Beck started signing to each other, it felt like a private discussion from the way Beck blushed, and Adam grinned at her.

"Hey," I guided Nicole to plop down next to me as we settled in on the picnic blanket, "I'd like to introduce you to my girlfriend, Nicole Young."

"I'm so excited to finally meet you," Beck bounced happily in her seat after shaking Nicole's hand. "I'm Beck. This is Adam."

"Hi," Nicole said. Adam shook her hand next.

"Thanks for hanging out with us," Beck said. "Gram was a big part of my life, which is how she became a big part of everyone else's lives, too. We try to visit her at least once a month." Beck stared at the tombstone lovingly. A picture of Susan was propped up against it, so she grabbed the frame and handed it to Nicole to admire.

"Oh, she's beautiful," Nicole sighed. The picture was a recent one of Susan Scott. Her white hair was tied in a knot haphazardly on her head. Her round glasses took up two-thirds of her face, and she smiled widely for the picture. A shawl she knitted herself was draped over her shoulders, and she was sitting in one of the hideous accent chairs that still resided in Courtney and Josh's place.

"She is," Beck agreed. Nicole handed the picture back to her, and Beck turned to face Nicole more directly. "Tell us about yourself! We haven't gotten to meet a lot of Taylor's partners in the past, so this is pretty exciting. Right?" She glanced up at Adam, sitting next to her, who nodded and gave Nicole a polite smile.

Nicole looked at me once before resting her hand on my thigh and asking, "What do you want to know?"

"Everything." Beck replied, "How did you two meet?"

"Mutual friends," we answered in unison.

Nicole giggled before clarifying, "I work with their teammates, and also a former client of theirs."

"Wow," Beck's hazel eyes widened, "Small world, huh?"

"Thank god," I replied, leaning back on my hands to stretch, "Otherwise who knew how long I would have continued fucking around."

Nicole gave me a chastising look, "There's nothing wrong with fucking around, Taylor."

"You're not wrong," I replied, leaning in close, "But now that I have you, it makes me want to throw up knowing that I could have gone my whole life without you in it."

Nicole raised a dark eyebrow at me, "You wouldn't have known better. It would have been the same as before you met me."

"Nicole," I shook my head at her, and leaned in close to her face, so that our foreheads were almost touching, "Logically, you're right. Emotionally, I don't like thinking about that. You're in my life now, and I'm keeping you."

Her dark eyes sparkled at my words, "Keeping me?"

"Yeah," I pecked her nose once and said, "For as long as you'll have me."

Her cheeks darkened with a blush as she started blinking rapidly. Her eyes shifted, acting as if she forgot about the company we shared.

"Oh, sorry—"

"Don't apologize," Beck raised her hands at us, "I get it. I totally get it."

Adam shifted closer to her, kissing the crown of her head as he studied the scenery around us.

"Oh, that reminds me—" I turned to face Beck head-on, "I'm sorry in advance."

Beck cocked her head to the side, "For what?"

"Because I'm probably going to marry Nicole." At my words, Nicole gasped and sat straighter, her head whipping toward me as I continued, "So you and Adam will be the only ones living in sin after that."

Nicole's eyes widened at me. "Did you just say, 'living in sin?'"

Beck threw her head back and cackled, then composed herself enough to say, "You don't have to apologize for that, T. Good god. Living in sin." Beck was still laughing, wiping a stray tear from her eye as she leaned into her boyfriend.

"Are you all religious?" Nicole asked the group.

"No." Beck shook her head, taking a deep breath, "Much to my parents' chagrin."

Nicole's mouth shaped into an *oh*, before she nodded in understanding.

"Married, huh?" Adam asked with a raised brow.

"Hell yeah," I glanced down at Nicole, who was blushing again, "Don't worry, I'm not proposing right now."

Nicole's brows raised, "So, when will you?"

I rolled my eyes at her, "I can't tell you that."

"What if *I* want to propose?"

I shrugged and said, "Then I'll say yes."

"Just like that?"

"Just like that."

Nicole scoffed, her cheeks holding their delicious blush, as she asked Beck and Adam how they met, and the conversation shifted.

I lay back on the picnic blanket, appreciating the peace of the cemetery. There were a few clouds left in the sky this morning that I gazed at as I listened to their conversation. Nicole would laugh at something Beck said every now and then, reminding me of that day at rugby that changed things for us all those weeks ago.

How quickly I went from "I'm probably never settling down" to "I can't wait until she wears my ring on her finger" within weeks. I still didn't care for weddings that much. But I knew Nicole did. It was a nugget of information I kept safe in my mental Nicole jar. Something I made sure to dig out when the time was right. Something I really, really wanted to do for her.

There wasn't going to be anyone else in my life.

No one ever had a hold on my heart like Nicole did.

Might as well throw a kickass party and make it legal.

The human experience never ceases to amaze me.

"Babe?" Nicole asked, leaning over me to get my attention. Her short black hair fell around her face, so I reached up to tuck some of it behind her ear.

"Yeah?"

"Nothing." Nicole smiled, before leaning down to press a kiss to my lips, "Just seeing if you're okay."

"I'm wonderful," I sighed, "I'm at peace."

Nicole bit her lip with a grin before pulling away and continuing her conversation with my friends.

I loved her.

Everything else seemed to be trivial compared to that knowledge.

Love was a powerful thing.

The elation of it was astounding. Knowing that there was one person in your corner, no matter what. Someone who fit me in all the ways I didn't realize I wanted. Someone I wanted to show off. Someone I wanted to settle in with every night.

Two people who could find comfort in each other.

My name is Taylor Desmond, and even though it was unexpected, I had exactly what I wanted.

THE END

Acknowledgments

First and foremost, thank you. Every time someone downloads or buys a book from me, it encourages me to keep following my dreams.

Second, I want to thank the sensitivity readers who helped me craft Taylor and Nicole's story. I wouldn't have had the ability to write this story at all if it weren't for sensitivity readers. In fact, I would have refused to write it entirely.

I had a lot of hesitation writing Taylor and Nicole's story. I kept going back and forth about it while I wrote WBAW and MBAM. I kept asking myself, am I really the person who should be writing a queer romance? Would publishing a queer romance unintentionally pull readers away from queer authors writing queer romance better (and more authentically) than I'll ever be able to?

On the other hand, what does it say about me if I actively avoid writing a queer romance? I didn't want readers to mistake the diverse characters in my stories as nothing more than tokens. A checkbox on a diversity list. Each one of my characters is created with a purpose. They have a distinct personality and goals.

A life.

Something to say.

I write diverse characters because it's weird (and unrealistic) to depict a world without diverse people. LGBTQIA+, BIPOC, and people who aren't straight, white, or cis exist everywhere else in the world. So, why wouldn't they be everywhere in fiction, too? Regardless of what the author identifies as.

To avoid further straight-splaining the need for diversity in literature, I'll end with this.

Thank you to the readers who fell in love with Taylor's character early on. To the readers who constantly checked in with me about when Taylor would finally get their own story. To the readers who have been here since day one, and to the readers who read this story before any of my others.

Thank you to my editors, proofreaders, friends, and family who have supported me in big and small ways.

I cannot say it enough, but I'll try.

So, thank you.

Also by Andrea Andersen

SUN STEER TECH SERIES:

WRITTEN BY A WOMAN

(Signe & Zaid's story)

MELTED BY A MAN

(Jacqueline & Leo's story)

WHAT IT MEANS SERIES:

WHAT IT MEANS TO BE WHOLE

(Beck & Adam's story)

WHAT IT MEANS TO BE BRAVE

(Courtney & Josh's Story)

WHAT IT MEANS TO BE FOUND

(Eloise & Logan's story)

About the Author

Andrea is originally from Oregon but now resides in southern California with her little family. When she isn't curled up on the couch writing love stories, she can be found rewatching her favorite TV shows or taking too many naps.

www.andreaandersen.com